OUT OF THE ASHES

An Anthology of Poetry and Prose
From Phoenix Writers' Circle

Dear Tina,

Hope you enjoy OUT OF THE ASHES

With love
Diana x

1

Copyright

Published by Lulu

ISBN: 978-1-291-32914-8(1)

Dedication

To all readers and writers everywhere – you make our world go round.

Chairman's Message
by Justine John

Phoenix Writers' Circle is a small group of creative and talented writers based in or near Dorking, Surrey. I first discovered the group when I was writing my first novel and found it inspirational – the chance to read my work aloud for the first time and have such experienced writers critique it helped me enormously. Not only that, but I finally had the opportunity to meet other writers and glean information, tips, advice.

After a short lapse in my writing habit, I returned as 'chairperson' in a bid to kick myself into shape and write another novel. We invited an agent to the group as a speaker, who shortly after chose to represent me, followed by a few others, and so I owe Phoenix a huge amount.

The meetings are a place where we can learn together, help and inspire each other, and enjoy everyone's unique talent. They are special to us all for various reasons, but most of all because we have found like-minded friends in whom we trust.

Here you will find a collection of our work, which we all sincerely hope you enjoy. We'd like to say a big thank you for picking up this book and reading it.

Foreword
by Tim Jenkins

A PHOENIX REBORN

Phoenix had been born after two earlier attempts to form a writing group in Bookham over 35 years ago, and because of its turbulent rebirths, it was called Phoenix, which was its name when I joined it in 1997/8. Whilst we had members who were not interested in writing poetry, the 80% who were also belonged to the newly formed Mole Valley Poets group. They decided to stick to just MVP which left us a group that just wrote prose.

I took over running the group in 2002. We had, for about eight years, a professional tutor, John Lemmon, from Surrey University which was the key to the survival and growth of Phoenix, with all genres welcome. Mole Valley Scriptwriters was born out of Phoenix and shared the same tutor for a while.

In 2001, we produced an anthology, but not again until this year, 20 years on. There were Phoenix Anthologies prior to 2001 but none since. So, it is about time that the creative genius of the group should be shared with the world and knowing the talented writers the group has, what this anthology offers is very special. It also showcases what the group, with its new and exciting management can offer writers. Certainly, a platform for success.

Contents

SHYNESS
by Alison Allen

Shyness was your first friend, speeding
your heels from the busy, peering world,
letting you play in silent freedom
shielded by her sullen stare.

In the playground her imperious hand
divided you from others. Voices chanting
One potato, two potatoes fell
with blunt thuds beside her magic veil.

Bully in the classroom, she swiped your seat
and stole your voice. *Not fair*. Words failed you.
If you raised your hand, you feared
she'd pin you down and leave you flailing.

These days she's subtle, a fragrance not a fist:
Like a terrier she'll rummage through the wardrobe
of your mind, strewing her rubbishy half-chewed
finds at the feet of your puzzled listeners.

She partners you at parties, her ice-cold hands
gripping your wine glass, stilling the smile
on your lips. Watch her knock back the drinks
as others retreat. She'll stop your mouth

as long as you let her, this piggy-back scold
who clings to your life. You deserve better.
Unpick those fingers, loosen her grasp,
See how she dwindles - her moment is past.

LOVE IN
THE MODERN AGE
by Peter Cates

I googled love, but it didn't say,
Of the pain I'd feel if you went away.
Memory banks so full of you,
Hard drive crash, long overdue.
Soul infected, by love's viral dart:
For there's no firewall on my heart.

LOVE'S JUNKY
by Peter Cates

My mind does twist as maudlin rhyme,
As I seek passage from happier times.
When our love was fierce and new,
And all others, we did eschew.
You were my heroine, drug of my desire,
Addiction grew with every day,
To fill my heart with fire.

THE MOTORCYCLE
by Peter Cates

I watch the road unfurl so fast.
In awe, as future hurtles into past.
Such music, from its vibrant need,
Too sate, this lust for manic speed.
With such elation in my grasp,
Down life's seeming endless road I blast.
My path I carve, through sweep and bend,
Wishing it to never end.
Once found, such thrills the mould is cast.
I am but striven to make it last,
Other pleasures now long past.
But should not caution temper flight,
The servant, can its master bite,
For single folly, can snuff life's light.
I watch the road unfurl so fast.
In awe, as future hurtles into past.

THE GREY DANCER IN THE TWILIGHT
by Richard Howard

"No, sir, I wouldn't go into the forest at dusk for any price. There are some things best left alone, undisturbed ~ secrets that belong only to Nature and the Savage Gods. Those who ignore the warnings never return and, believe me, there have been many over the years ~ no trace ever found."

I remember these words well. They came from an old forester I met during one of my evening strolls at the Summer Solstice. The light was just beginning to fade and I remember the look of fear on his weathered face. He had spent his life in the forest and the legends and superstitions associated with it were as certain to him as the sun that rose each morning. I was surprised at meeting him. I'd wandered in that forest many times before and never met a soul. Then there he was, standing motionless in front of me. Deep in thought, I'd almost walked straight into him and was startled by his sudden appearance. After apologising and reorientating myself, we fell into conversation, and anxious not to seem unfriendly, I told him of my lifelong love of the forest and how I often ventured there seeking peace and tranquility to escape an aggressive and fractured world. I spoke, too, of that particular enchantment when the light changes perceptibly at the hours of dawn or dusk. He listened in silence as I enthused about those magical moments of dawn when creeping light spills across the forest floor, penetrating the foliage and rekindling from slumber the myriad forms of life. But when I spoke of dusk, even as dusk was then approaching, he became perceptibly uneasy as if he had witnessed something of which he dared not speak.

Convinced that one so identified with nature would have some fascinating stories to tell, I pressed him to say something of his experiences. Like myself, he had grown up close to the forest and had sought and welcomed its tranquility since childhood. He spoke of many enchanting encounters with animals which, growing accustomed to his familiar and unthreatening presence, were emboldened to approach him, allowing him to regard them almost as pets. He knew the hiding places of every species, where to find them, when to leave them alone, and all the phases of their evolution. He told me of a wounded fox he'd once found, how he'd nursed it back to health and how, thereafter, it always came to greet him. He was certain that on one occasion it had saved him from danger by delaying him long enough to avoid a falling tree.

Not entirely convinced, I listened but said nothing to undermine his belief, and taking account of his openness to such a possibility, I ventured on the subject of myths and wondered, perhaps a little too rashly, whether in all his years he had experience of other more elusive creatures. I had in mind those usually found among the pages of legend and folklore, and consistently depicted in paintings of almost every culture over the centuries, such fleeting and magical figures as fauns, centaurs, satyrs, nymphs and unicorns, or perhaps even Pan himself. I wasn't explicit but he understood my meaning instantly and eyed me with suspicion. When I then conjectured that those magical times of changing light seemed to me most felicitous in conjuring such unexpected visions, he stepped away and, raising his voice, as much in fear as indignation, he made that pronouncement which I've never forgotten.

With the first signs of dusk now evident, he turned and walked hastily away as he repeated the words: "Those who ignore the warnings never return," and vanished as unexpectedly as he had first appeared.

It was usually at dusk that the sense of enchantment was most mysterious, especially so on moonless nights, when without the lunar light there was, it seemed, a certain 'glow' that emanated from everything around me. At first, I presumed this was simply the effect of my eyes growing accustomed to the darkness, but there were moments when my vision seemed even clearer than in normal daylight. And on one such occasion, what I saw astounded me.

It was one damp autumn evening. I'd wandered down to the woods in a state of contemplation to ponder in solitude some question or other that had been preoccupying me. The light was fading and a dense mist hovered a foot or two above the ground. Then suddenly I was aware of someone else, an almost translucent figure some distance away that seemed to rise up out of the mist into a clearing where, with arms outstretched and an almost elfin-like agility, it began silently to move as if performing some strange ritual dance before vanishing into the twilight. The scene lasted little more than a minute but was etched in my memory ever afterwards. During those brief moments, time was suspended and when the figure vanished, I was left peering into the gloom, eager to catch just one more glimpse of whatever it was that had so captivated my attention.

My eyes straining against the rising mist and encroaching darkness, I was suddenly struck by the silence of the forest, as if every living creature had stilled itself until that mysterious intruder was safely beyond reach. Against that suspension of activity, all I could hear were random drops of water falling from the trees onto a carpet of dead leaves, sounds that emphasised the depth of that haunted silence. After several minutes everything was normal again and reluctantly I turned to go, taking with me an unexplained image that urged me to return. And return I did, frequently. For the ensuing five evenings I went to the forest at the same time, hoping to repeat my experience and gain a clearer perception of what I'd seen. But it was not to be. Not, that is, until I found myself there by chance the following year at the Spring Equinox.

As always, the surge of energy at spring ~ the burgeoning of trees, the intensity of green and the bustling activity of wildlife ~ fills the air with a sense of renewed hope that is irresistible to anyone attuned to nature and nourished by its spell. Drawn back to the forest, my vision of the previous autumn had dimmed a little but was not forgotten and, given the significance of the day, I dared to wonder whether I would once again witness that strange figure in the twilight.

No sooner had I wondered when I was instantly transfixed. In a clearing some several yards from where I stood, lit by the evening light, a shadowy figure emerged from the trees and, just as before, proceeded to dance with an elegance and agility that suggested a distinct purpose, though what that purpose was remained a mystery. On this occasion, I was able to observe for far longer than previously, during which the dancer's movements seemed to me to beckon, to lure, even to seduce. I remained perfectly still, attention fixed, lest the slightest move might cause the scene to evaporate.

I remembered the forester's warning, uttered with such gravity and fear, and yet, nevertheless, I was increasingly tempted to take the risk of moving closer to the apparition that now captivated my senses with increasingly eloquent movements and a choreography that seemed joyous and inviting. Fully expecting the dancer's sudden disappearance, I took a cautious step forward and as I did so, the only change was in colour. The greyness of that figure, silhouetted against the fading evening light, was enhanced with shimmering peacock colours that made this phantasm appear ever more solid and real. Entranced, I risked a second step and as I did so, the colours of the dancer became enriched and more enticing. In the same moment, the sky beyond grew strangely brighter, completely at odds with the hour and the evening light. Despite every graceful movement of the dancer, who now began to retreat, I once again became aware of the depth of silence that lay over the scene, and I realised that my choice was either to follow, or to remain where I stood and break the spell. I had waited so long to see this apparition again, and yet now, with that sombre voice echoing in my mind, I hesitated. 'Those who ignore the warnings never return.'

But not wanting to lose sight of the dancer, I moved impulsively forward ~ an almost involuntary act ~ as the figure continued to retreat. Recklessly throwing caution to the wind, I hastened after it and, as I did so, somewhere in the depth of my awareness, I understood what it was to be entranced. To 'entrance' creates an entrance. And so it was that as I followed, I lost all sense of time and entered another world. The once fading light of evening became a new dawn. Light enlightened me, illuminating mysteries I had pondered all my life. The dancer vanished into brilliance, leaving me stranded in a landscape of light. All perspectives changed and as my senses adjusted, I found myself at the edge of a different forest inhabited by many animals with which I was familiar and others I could never have imagined, all of which seemed tame and unafraid. I glimpsed, also, several of those mythical beings I had seen in paintings and read about in stories that many dismissed as fanciful. And among them I saw people of every culture in mutual harmony, conversing with each other and communing with the richness of life that surrounded them. In the distance, merging into even brighter light, were vistas so sublime they defied all powers of description and appeared to me, eternal. At the same moment, I experienced a sense of profound peace.

A moment later, I felt a presence at my side and turned to see a young woman of extreme beauty. She greeted me with a knowing smile. Then she pointed in the direction from which I had arrived and for a moment a dark grey tunnel opened before us. She guided me towards the entrance. It was my opportunity to return to the life I had left behind. But as we approached, all I could hear were screams of anger, cries of fear, voices in argument, and the clash of eternal conflict that reminded me of that aggressive and fractured world from which I had so often sought refuge. A single word formed in my mind, perhaps placed there by my guide: Hell.

As we turned back towards the light, I remembered the forester's warning and his fear of the unknown. It saddened me, for the unknown is knowable. But I now also knew precisely why 'no one ever returned'. If only I could tell him. Perhaps one day he will overcome his fear.

STABAT MATER DOLOROSA
by A A Marcoff

they came out of the wind like the north: soldiers: the brutals – with helmet, armour, blade: never look into the eye of a killer – it is dark, dead, hollow, black: something had stirred in the cosmos as though the sun were somehow changed, the sky darkening now and now: people covered their ears, for those screams were too piercing, searing, cutting as a knife into the fabric of the mind...

clouds passed over like whole eras of history, these moments broken as time itself, and the man-whipped man came along the road, and carried a wooden cross that was heavy as the Earth: and he was wearing a white robe: he was wearing light itself: a robe that was simple and plain in the nature of things: and his mother saw him there, watched as he stumbled, almost tripping over stones that were hard on his bare feet, and her hair flowed down her white neck like water, and she was like a swan, with wings of white sky:

in the beginning
was the Word –
the flight of a swan
brings wings to the world,
endlessly

and she was full of sorrow now, white with tears, her eyes wide with pity: he was her child sublime: and she followed, her head bent now, the procession heading to a barren place, which was called golgotha, the place of the skull, and she could not watch any more: heard the coarse shouts, voices raised in mockery, heard the whips and the lashing, heard the hammering of nails, his body being broken on a cross of heavy wood, and the nails were the ripping of the daylight and the coming of shadows to the desert: and there was blood: she was no longer aware of the passage of time, and she waited there, standing, numbed, blank, as the sun disappeared from the hill, and she felt the stones underfoot in her emotion, everything dark for a period: and no-one knew why, for it was still daytime: and she waited there, standing in the sublime, and she heard him cry out, and he sounded abandoned and looked outstretched there wide as a bird, and she wanted to speak to him, but could not...

the quiet radiance
of his eyes –
slow gold shadows
on
silence

and she saw a centurion known as Longeus, a blind man who did not see with his eyes but saw with his mind what was transpiring, a man who had insight and knowledge: he knew a story of a star, and a tree, and a tomb, and a garden where that man would appear again as illumination and physical presence and as radiance: and though he was full of sorrow, the blind man took a spear, and pierced the man's heart, to relieve his suffering at the end of things and in the deeper course of history, and then the blood of the man ran down the shaft of the spear, and touched the blind centurion, and suddenly, in a storm of light, he saw again, his eyes opened up and he was not blind any more:

Good Friday:
travelling
through time & light –
swallows
at the Crucifixion

and the mother watched, as the spirit of her son rose like white smoke into sky – she could see that, see it like a shaft that cut into the textures of the sky, and lit up the darkness, as the sun returned in visionary power, white and bright and shining through the veil of darkness, which was torn now, like dream: and the first day came and went: and the second day came and went: and there was creation, out of the complex, from the night, and so on the third day they all heard a voice from the dawn of time speaking, 'let there be light!':

a light gospel dawn:
sunrise
in the valleys
of
the world

and she saw the coming of a child in the east of the land, child that was the structure of time, a theology of light: and it was as if the tree of the crucified had blossomed into pink, here within the solar system, in the affirmation and intimation of eternity and breath: there was a crucifix of light: and it was immensity in the mother's mind: and her being was filled suddenly, as though with endless space and song, a simple song of the Earth, of worlds: aria of arias, pure voice as clear as the sky, pure voice as clear as running water in a brook, as she saw birds reappear in the silence of trees, a rising sun in their song, as a river of water ran through her mind, a river of life...

and there are white swans here, opening their wings, outstretched as the rays of the sun, wide as the world: and the mother glides there upon the waters, and he is there too, swan of swans, wings like gospels that flow into the moment, and he moves by her side, in parallel, in parable, and his wings are galaxies of feather and glide, and the wake of the swan is the rhythm of the breeze, currency of gospel and word and bird and vitality, simple as a song, its shape clear as daylight: there is a great halo on the land around, and on the riverbank apostles walk in their freedom, and they are lateral, structural, and roam amongst lilies in the fields, speaking now the tongue of reality, moving among vineyards and gold and a place of corn growing into harvest: a girl from a pearl holds a single sunflower in her hand: and swan on swan, they merge now like parable with the sun, in the perception of our eyes, immaculate, serene, as everything flows like water and the future and the current of the mind, and two swans move in the fullness of time, as in a dreaming of the stunning of the sun:

a world
beyond theology
the river flows
into light
like a swan

in the sowing of the dawn – the seeds of reality, its various strands woven with energy: and all shall be well, and all manner of thing shall be well – visions of the houses of stone and the structure of stars: there was the breaking of a chord in the distant past, and a latent atmosphere of rose and ultraviolet – there in the cosmic glow: and suddenly they all heard the sound of the sun...

APRIL
by Jill Benson

I was born in the growing month,
When the land turns green and pink and white,
And the blackthorn crowns the privet hedge.
When the beech - silk of the woods -
Puffs lime-green clouds
From trees that tower
And ride steep slopes
On tiptoe,
Where the soil is thin.

I was born in the growing month...

SEA AT SIDMOUTH
by Jill Benson

Towering, sinister, swooping cliffs.
Sea churning red below,
Making songs out of seaweed and shipwrecks.
Hidden depths, watery deaths.
Sea is a chameleon:
From silk to shimmering satin,
Thence to glass....
All in one day.

BLOODY SEAGULLS AT DAWN!
by Jill Benson

A ragged rabble
Of seagulls.
A chorus of discontent
Drag the new day,
Kicking and screaming,
To my door.

DEADLY PERSUASION
by Kenneth Clelland

Many years ago, so the legend runs, there was a sage who lived high in the mountains and all the folk from miles around, who were troubled, would climb the mountain to consult this wise man. He would sit and listen quietly to their troubles. He would then give them good advice and send them home to make what they would of it.

Some would listen and do nothing.

Some would listen and select to do only what they found easy.

Some would listen and follow his advice exactly.

The latter always profited from the advice they had received.

But there was a mystery surrounding the wise man that all the folk would talk about. For it seemed that the Sage had always been there. Even the oldest in the village remembered their parents, grandparent and great grandparents talking of him in the same way. It seemed that there had always been a sage there. Yet from time to time, every forty years or so, he would change his appearance. It was said that he became young again. And his new look was always similar to one of the young men from the surrounding villages who would strangely disappear from the village.

Now it came to pass that one day a young man from the village of Tolas (meaning beloved of the gods) climbed the mountain to the Sage's shack to talk with him. He had done this many times before. He had no problem in particular; it was just that he found the old man's conversation and wise words pleasant to listen to and it appeared that the old man also found the young man's company agreeable.

As usual he arrived at the shack a little out of breath after his climb and was greeted warmly at the door by the wise old man.

"Come in and sit down, my son," he said to the youth.

"Thank you, Wise Father" said the youth as he crossed the small room to a seat at the foot of the Sage's chair. It was traditional in the village to address the Sage as 'Wise Father', for it was very much in those terms that they regarded him.

"Today" said the old man when they were both seated, "I have something special to discuss with you."

"To discuss with me, Wise Father?" replied the youth incredulously, for he felt very privileged that the old man should have chosen him to discuss his business with.

"Yes, my son, with you. First, I must ask you some questions but fear not," he said reassuringly," There will be no questions too hard for you to answer."

"I will do the best that I can," said the young man.

"Knowing you as I do," the Sage continued, "I would expect no less. Let us begin. First tell me, what do the people in the villages say of my great age."

"The people of my village marvel at it. Some say that you steal the bodies of young men; that you become them and they die. But others in the village scold them, saying, that this cannot be, for the Wise Father is good and the stealing of bodies is so evil that the suggestion is absurd."

The old man smiled and then asked "How do those that have such trust in me answer the question?"

"I am one of those that trust you," replied the young man reverentially "And that is sufficient in itself. I ask no more."

The old man put a hand on the lad's shoulder. "But, if I was to tell you my secret, you would listen I expect." The old man's eyes seem to shine as he spoke.

"If you were to tell me your secret, I would respect that privilege and preserve it."

"You have answered well my son and have therefore earned the right to be made privy to one of the oldest secrets of mankind." For a moment the old man stared into the hearth as if there were a fire there and he was divining great truths from the glowing heart of the fire. Turning his eyes to the boy again he began. "The story of the great tower is my starting point. Are you acquainted with it my son?"

The young man reflected for a few moments then said. "I think so. The story tells of a time long ago, when all the people of the world united to build a great tower to reach to the heavens. The gods seeing this were annoyed that mankind had become so strong and cast a spell on them so that they all spoke different languages. This brought such chaos and disunity that the work on the tower had to stop."

"Yes" said the old man, "that is the tale to which I refer, my son. But it is a tale invented by man to hide his own shortcomings. For, I ask you, what wise god would plant disunity among men who showed such promise. The tale though does have some small element of truth as it tells of a downfall of mankind.

"My secret goes back to the days before this fall, when man was first learning to unite with his fellow man. A priesthood grew up in the Great Mountains. Over the years they learnt through study, prayer and meditation many great spiritual mysteries. The most important of these was the achievement of a level of spiritual communion that no longer required the spoken word to communicate. Mind would speak straight to mind. Over the centuries the entire priesthood learnt to think as one, however great their physical distance. Under the instruction of the priesthood, to a limited degree, the people also developed some ability to do this. Out of this the power was born the minds total control over matter. With the guidance of the priests using their will to bind the whole, a mighty chain of minds existed around the earth. Nothing could stand in the way of such power.

"But a chain is as strong as its weakest link. Sadly, pride infected the priesthood and soon there were factions in conflict and the collapse into chaos began. But within the priesthood there was a group that was determined to retain spiritual integrity. They went into secret seclusion and continued to perfect their lives while watching the world's decline into anarchy. Finally, at the nadir, with mankind reduced to savagery, this select group went out into the world to serve the people as I do and to watch and await the moment when mankind rediscovers their spirituality. But this new priesthood was small and aging and without action would have become extinct. The answer lay in another great spiritual power that they had developed. That was the ability to merge two beings as one. This preserved all the wisdom of the centuries; The old discarding their bodies to merge with the young. But as there were now no young priests, suitable young men from outside the priest hood were invited to become hosts to old priests and therefore part of the priesthood themselves.

"Because you are an especially wise young man," he said holding the boy's shoulder with a talon grip, "I am offering you the chance to become the new priest; to sit as I have and hundreds before me to help guide the people."

"But I have not got your wisdom and would never be able to offer the advice that you can," said the young man.

"Surely you understand that you will be joined by this union through me to hundreds of priests who are already a part of me and linked to all the others around the world. From this will come the wisdom."

Suddenly terror filled the young man. He could see that the village doubters were right. It seemed that death was close one way or the other.

He spotted a fine jeweled dagger on the small table next to him. Trying to control the fear in his voice he said quickly, "Who could possibly refuse such an honour, Wise Father," but reaching secretly he grabbed the dagger. He now believed he was fighting for not only his life but his soul. Standing with the knife behind him, he turned to face the Sage, "I am honoured by this opportunity beyond all reason. I am totally unworthy of such distinction, but as I believe it is impossible to deny you, Wise Father, I must therefore give you the only reply I can."

Dropping to his knees before the Sage he drove the knife into the old man's heart. He was shocked at the way the blood rushed out to cover his hand. But as he watched the blood, it disappeared like water into sand as if it were soaking into his flesh. He then heard a familiar voice in his head say, "I am so glad you decided to join us."

FAMILY VALUES
by John Lemmon

I once tried to poison my parents
By putting disinfectant in their tea.
I was eight.
They convinced themselves that I
Had been trying to clean the cups
And had, as usual, got it wrong.
They didn't think that every slap,
Every stroke of the broken violin bow
My father used as a cane
Had earned its compound interest of hate.
The first time he caned me my father
Bent me over a chair and said,
'This is going to hurt me more than it hurts you'.
Bollocks.
You can sin by platitude
Even if you are a card-carrying Christian,
Even when you teach a Sunday school class
And come home to brutalize your own child.
My father later committed suicide -
I doubt it was from guilt.
He drove off in the middle of the night
And I watched him disappear into the darkness.
Next day coming home on the bus
From East Croydon to Sanderstead I caught
Myself praying that he had gone off and killed himself.
Which he had. It was the only prayer of mine
That God ever answered. Through all those years
He watched and listened in detached silence.
I never forgave him.

BERMUDA
by Nora George

And she said – tell me what you like
He said – oh I like it all

It began before that
They were talking in a restaurant
When she met him she didn't think ooh
He looked nice, kind of average really
But he was talking like a storyteller
With his words he created magical images
In her mind
She enjoyed listening and she could imagine
All the things he said
It was very interesting to her
So she was thinking, yes – I like you
The things you say
The things he chose to reveal
Intelligence and sensitivity
And a sense of wonder
As she listened a pang of desire
Surprised her like a leap in her heart
She made an involuntary sound but so quietly
It passed un-noticed
Though there were several more
So, sitting behind him on the bike going back, in the warm
evening
She teased herself
She put her lips close, so close to his skin
On his back, his shoulder

Nearly touching, nearly a kiss
She knew he did not know about this
She left and said goodbye

Another evening alone with him later
They drank tea on the verandah
And skirted a little with each other
The possibility of a kiss, a touch
But it passed by, she left

When they were snorkelling in Church Bay
She put sun lotion on his back
As gently as she dared
For as long as she dared
Uncertain, she did not want to give a signal
But she wanted to touch

It was later back in his room
Outside an electrical storm thundered
He offered to give her a massage
She lay on his floor
And with fragrant oil
He massaged her back
Her neck
Wonderfully, beautifully, tenderly
He spoke in a low voice, almost a whisper
So not to break the spell
The soft evening light
Made them look beautiful
After a long time
When she was in another consciousness
Created by the rain, the light, his touch, the rhythm
The excitement of his touch, his closeness

He leant forward
And kissed her back, at the top
By her neck
His lips just gently brushing her skin
Satisfying her longing for his kiss
She half turned and lifted her head
To kiss his lips his face
To touch him with her fingers

He massaged her legs, her feet, her toes
He kissed her toes
Then she lay on her back
He knelt by her head
And gently touched her face
Her arms, her body
Her breasts
Her body was warm and fragrant
The oil was absorbed into her skin
Desire for him grew stronger
But they did not make love

Another day in his room he said
I feel as if I've got hungry hands

When she looked at him
His lips formed as if to kiss, as he touched her
Their shape transmitted his desire
He smiled
And her body responded to all the cues he gave
She could see it in his face
Feel it in his touch
In his rhythmic caress and body moving

When they made love
She felt as if in heaven
Transported by him to another realm
She felt she could lose consciousness with pleasure and
desire

One morning after they made love in the house
Where she stayed
She looked at his body
At his beautiful black curls
Where her blood lay glistening
Look oh look, it looks like rubies, she said.

When the time
Came for her to leave
It came suddenly
Uncertainty crept in
He had said – call me from the airport
But he was working
They could not really say anything
It was just to say goodbye.

THE PHOTOGRAPH
by Justine John

This eerie building no longer stands,
Except in a picture, I hold in my hand.
Ruinous walls that once were white, its roof with holes that allow the light
To pool on grass and dust and brick, where beetles scuttle and spiders quick.
Who lived here once upon a time, I question simply, one more time?
A lady stands in front, her arm
Around a young boy, with appealing charm,
And a little girl too, no more than ten.
She smiles into the camera lens.
The photo, circa seventy-two? My family went to see the view
of the beach below, the waves so high, thrusting forward, back, to justify
The salty air and sky so blue,
The sun ablaze, a golden hue.
I found a shell there, in the sand,
But this eerie building no longer stands.

This eerie building no longer stands,
In its place a restaurant, much in demand
Fresh shellfish from the sea below, and waiters scuttle to and fro.
Red velvet seats where diners whisper, music flows, light as a whisker.
The son too is gone, in another place.

He fought his battle with such little grace;
Assumptions kept but barely outed, and secret thoughts that fair amounted
To shame and guilt, which could not fly, instead became a lullaby.
The mother, dear, was rich in love
But sore and bitter, too much to prove.
When fate it took a lengthy turn, which challenged her from stem to stern
She also took a journey there, and with her tale of her love affair.

The only one standing left to see
Just me, a daughter with a memory
of heart and soul, it was sorrow-free
And there, existing, as if in my hand.
But this eerie building no longer stands.

THE LADY IN THE LANE
by Wendy Freeman

I see her every day, wandering the lanes between the villages. She looks so sad, so lonely. She always wears the same brown corduroy jacket and a leather shoulder bag, although I don't know why she would need the bag, the village shop closed down years ago. Sometimes as I ride past, I ring my bell and wave to her. She doesn't notice me of course. We are on different sides of a divide. There are a lot more cars whizzing up and down the lanes now; it used to be quieter. The drivers just pass her without noticing.

She walks whatever the season or the weather; in the heat of June and July, past the fields of buttercups and lazy cattle, and in late summer when the hedgerows glisten with blackberries. There is a cottage by the little stone bridge where it happened. Its garden has damson trees overhanging the road, in August the fruits plop down heavily and leave a squashy mess in the road. The widowed lady who lives there used to let me and my children pick the damsons and fill our bags with them. She even walked every day last winter too, although it was such a hard one, still she walked, her elbows brushing the snow that rested on the spiky branches.

I long to speak to her, but I can't. I wish I could tell her that it's all right. She can't hear me of course, although once I thought she sensed my presence, and maybe, I'm not sure, but maybe, just momentarily, we made eye contact. Some people are like that aren't they? They can see things other people can't. I wish she could find peace; I wish we could both find peace, but we probably never will.

The whole thing is almost forgotten now, apart from by our families, my children and her husband. I think Susan, the cottage owner, remembers it too, I often see her standing by the window, just looking out into the lane. 'The Daily Post' reported it at the time, they showed photos of both of us.

Then it was no longer news. We are both forgotten. Sometimes she lingers at that spot on the bridge, probably reliving that terrible moment which took one life and changed the other.

She used to drive a nice car then, a big, new car, when she had a good job in town. She doesn't drive now of course. I had never learnt, so I cycled everywhere. It kept me fit. I remember that morning my son mentioned that my rear lamp was on the blink.

It was January, late afternoon, and almost dark. It had been trying to snow all day. As it was cold, I was wearing a woolly hat instead of a helmet; would it have made any difference? I was hurtling down the hill past the cottage as her car came round the bend and skidded. It happened in the fluttering of a snowflake. I was catapulted in the air and landed on my head, leaving a squashy mess of damson juice.

In the last few moments of my life, I heard her voice, screaming, hysterical. I felt her hand touch my head briefly, then recoil and pull back. There was another voice, a man's, it must have been another driver who stopped to help. I think he was phoning for an ambulance, but by the time it arrived I had long departed.

It was a freak accident, even my children didn't blame her, but she blames herself, and I'm sorry for that. She has nothing now, no job, no car, no life. I suppose she walks up and down the lane because she has nothing else to do with her time. All I can do is watch her sadly, poor tormented lady in the lane.

FOUR-LETTER WORD
by Sally-Claire Fadelle

I am a maker
of strings for tongues.
To sing,
to wrap around
to lick and linger,
peruse or misuse,
at will.
Meaning in metaphor
abstract of pure fact
distilled in mind's eye,
for what is it to die,
to love, hate
or cry?

Lie with me
amidst Autumn's leaves
orange and pink.
Bright Summer trees
or frost-bitten Winter
Chilled,
frozen earth
till Spring renews, rebirth.

No rhyme
sometimes.

Words woven in stanzas
to touch; to tickle,
for faint heart or fickle
I meddle and mess with your mind
concerning the plight,
the pain and pleasure
of humankind,
then just as I make,
so, I take ~ you to new places
in lines and spaces.
Words defying time,
 universal
fill the vapid void
like butterflies
flit ~ fluttering
from flower to field
yield.
Perplexion
infusing
fallacious thoughts
I bring you
freedom,
inner peace;
sleep.

Complexities of life
I bring you night
your inner eyelids
a cinematic screen ~
of dreams,
mine ~ borrowed...
...stolen.
passed on

in your locution
free takeaway…
…after all I give you
you call me quite simply
a four-letter word…

POET.

THE FOURTEEN-YEAR BLUES
by Andrew Jackson

She looked good in red. If I had my choice, she'd have been in blue. But I missed that. I missed the pigtails; the way her thumb would pucker with wrinkles after she sucked it all night. The best friend who ditched her for a sleepover at the cool kid's house. She wouldn't even call me dad this morning, as we shared a fry up in the café down the road from my place. Nicole would have given me hell about clogging up our daughter's arteries. But she'd run it off. PE was period three.

I knew that much.

I tipped a wave over the wheel as I watched her shuffle into the side gate of the school, the tall blonde girl swallowed by the sea of greasy teenagers. Her green backpack lingered a moment longer. Did she always shuffle? Or was that a new development?

Some jumpy mother gave me a toot from the horn of her BMW, the chrome grille glittering in the cool morning air. I ignored her.

My phone buzzed in my pocket as I watched the kids pour in. A wild-haired boy was doing a wheelie through the crowd, ringing his bell and stooping to spank a girl who stepped aside at the last moment. They expelled you for that now, I heard.

The mother behind me was passing my window now, shooting daggers over her twin boys' heads. I continued ignoring her.

The text was from Derek. He'd put his name into my phone alongside a little smiley face I didn't know how to remove or replace with a middle finger.

Ellie – Eleanor could text now. Apparently, it was old hat. Which is why she didn't do it. Or at least didn't text me. It struck me as strange. That the last hurdle to cross, the most intimate connection, came through a phone. I wondered if she texted about me.

I read Derek's text, sighed, and threw the phone onto the passenger seat as I turned across the stream of traffic and back onto the high street.

My parole officer had done me the ultimate indignity. He'd found me a job. I'd listed myself as "freelancer" whenever any of those church do-gooders had popped in with their milky tea and stale rich tea biscuits; the height of luxury for block E. We were supposed to refrain from telling the old biddies what we thought of Jesus while the screws stood three deep in the prison chapel. Little Ed had to be excused after adding his own milk to the tea. He'd done two weeks in segregation for that. And I'd done four days for laughing. But I wasn't laughing now. I turned into Raven Court, crossing a roundabout that reminded me I needed new suspension, and headed left onto Fairfield Avenue. Two storeys, two cars, two point five kids and a mortgage. Sometimes two lovers, one through the backdoor. The suburbs I'd dreamed of a lifetime ago.

I parked outside the Starbucks bulging from the wall of the job centre like some hopeful tumour. The parking was free, the coffees weren't. I doubted Derek was feeling generous.

My parole officer sat in the back corner, paunch swelling his black turtleneck. His perennial clipboard was tapping the table to the beat of Elton John's Rocket Man, playing softly through the headphones of some spotty kid working on an essay and a cappuccino.

"Simon," Derek's red face split into a shark's grin as I took the seat opposite him. He had a tall hot chocolate loaded with marshmallows in front of him. I had a tepid water. He tapped his watch. "Running a bit late, are we?"

Derek was about forty. Which made him a good decade younger than me. I was pleased to see further white in his dark sideburns. Perhaps it stopped me throwing my water in his face.

"School rush, you know how it is," I grunted.

"Ah," he tapped his nose. "I do, I do." He looked thoughtful. "Still, I wouldn't have thought you'd be tardy today." He tapped his pen against the clipboard. The sound cut through the aroma of his drink and the mumbled conversation of the patrons like a playground whistle. My eyes involuntarily rolled over it. Twenty years ago, I could have ripped it out of his fat hand, flipped it, and buried it to the hilt in his throat. Would have, if I'd been paid to. But that pen had the power to send me back to the slammer with a flick of his wrist. And the bastard knew it. Also, it was blue. A shame to spoil it.

"Sorry," I said, looking away from his maddening smile, "won't happen again."

"See that it doesn't, please." He tapped his clipboard again. "It wouldn't look good, you know."

I focused on a flyaway Sainsburys bag outside the window and tried not to think about an assault charge.

"Anyway," Derek clapped and slurped his hot chocolate. "How was she today?"

"Fine." I turned and looked at him. I should have shaved before coming out. Two day's growth sat on my cheeks like the chocolate sprinkles in his drink. At least I'd showered.

"I must say, Nicole and Stephen, was it?" He peeked over the rim of his cup. He knew damned well it was. I stayed quiet. Derek looked disappointed. "They've been particularly good about all this. Letting her spend every third weekend at your flat. How is she settling in?"

"Fine," I said again.

"You might have to give me more than that," he said. "There's safeguarding to think about ..."

"She's safe," I said. "Nicole says so, Stephen says so," I heard the venom as I pronounced the art gallery owner's name and hated myself for it. "And I say so."

"Ah, but what does young Eleanor say?" Derek reclined backwards. I watched his jeans stretching, hoping the button was about to pop and humiliate him. No such luck.

"Not a lot. Still." I looked at my water, so I didn't have to see his fucking grin.

"There, there," Derek said. "She'll come round. Not every teenager has a jailbird daddy, after all."

I bit my lip.

"So, are you excited about today?" Derek said after a moment, savouring his barb.

"Ecstatic," I said.

"That's my man!" He drummed plump fingers on the serving tray. "Did you bring your uniform?"

I shrugged my shoulder in the bag strap. Derek took that for assent.

"Good man," He slapped my arm. "And you can drive there okay?"

"Last I checked," I said.

"Just think, it's not much different to cleaning the showers, but you actually get paid! How exciting is that?"

"Turning cartwheels," I said.

"Well, get out all that sarcasm right here," Derek laughed.

"No time for that on the job. How are you finding it all?"

"Mop, bucket, floor," I said.

"Precisely," Derek nodded. "Wash away your sins, day by day. Soon we won't even need to meet every week." He looked around conspiratorially before whispering. "I'm going to miss it."

"I bet you will," I said. Derek laughed and made a note on his clipboard.

But he was right about one thing. I did enjoy the job. In a way.

The sky was grey as I drove across town, the first spots of rain pattering off the windscreen. It made me anxious. Winter light the same shade as my puke-stained mattress and the tracksuit I'd worn for fourteen years. The shade of nonentity, the shade of 6 a.m. with a screw rattling his truncheon through the railings, the shade of lumpy porridge and no hope.

It was too much to hope for the sun in mid-February. But it wasn't the sun I wanted. I dug my fingers into my bag as I turned into the leisure centre car park. The soft blue material of my new uniform soothed me. I lifted it out, pulled it to my nose and sniffed it. Washing powder and the tobacco I'd kicked last month when Eleanor told me it stank, and she wanted to go home. I'd hoped she'd meet me halfway. But so far, she just sat in her room with the door locked, talking on her phone. I felt awkward about confronting her, so I just lay on the sofa watching Friends and twitching for a fag. Nicole said it would take time. Her compassion was harder than Derek's glee.

I sat there for a while, fighting the panic and the thousand-yard stare. Thanks to the uniform, I won.

The girl on reception was young, red-haired, with a spider's web tattoo inside her left wrist. She looked at me with a mixture of curiosity and disgust as I shuffled up to the desk, passing a sweaty guy coming out of the gym with a towel over his shoulder. He was about the size I used to be.

"Clocking in," I nodded at her, expecting her to tap her keyboard and let me through the turnstiles. The gatekeeper of purgatory.

She hesitated a moment, eyes searching my face. I wondered if she'd been told what I'd done. Maybe I made good break room gossip. I'd been charged with almost everything back on that prehistoric cold morning. They'd let me put my jeans on, but that was about it. Aggravated assault, GBH, possession of a firearm, reckless driving, tax evasion. They'd even done me for the ounce of weed next door. But the big one, accepting money for a contract killing, had piled up the years like a stack of American pancakes.

I grinned hesitantly at the girl. She was probably wondering how this shrivelled old man in his blue jeans and dirty jacket could intimidate a hamster.

"We open at 11:30," she told me unnecessarily. "You need to be done by then."

"Uh-huh," I said. She unlocked the turnstiles.

"Oh," she said as I turned. "and Mr Baxter said you can't park in the staff car park anymore. You're not um …"

I looked over my shoulder at her. She at least looked guilty. And maybe a little hopeful. That I'd rip off her boss's toupee and make him eat it. But she had the wrong man.

"No worries," I said.

I had to change in little more than a broom closet. The musty darkness and the smell of cleaning fluid brought back memories of lights out, the air pregnant with howls unuttered. I dressed quickly, my heart thundering in my chest.

I felt better when I got to the pool.

The hall was long and wide, mostly dominated by the main pool, thirty metres long. My trainers squeaked on the wet beige tile as I wheeled the cart along behind me. The smell of chlorine was strong, and one of the overhead speakers, set high in the ceiling, was crackling with occasional static.

I liked this room the best. I always meant to save it for last, but I always gave in to temptation. To my right, swing doors opened onto the smaller kid's pool. A blur of orange rubber was visible through the translucent glass. A duck float, maybe. Which I should have stuck Eleanor in and felt her little hands slide panic-stricken over my forearms. That room was harder.

I whistled faintly as I worked, conscious of the bay windows of the viewing gallery above me. Baxter always seemed to find an excuse to be up there whenever I was working. The top of his sandy headpiece was nodding, phone pressed to his ear. Perhaps he was worried I was going to steal the water.

It was tempting. I worked slowly and methodically, picking fragments of nail and strands of hair out of the grates lining the pool's edge. I mopped up sticky patches and hoovered dry bits with the little handheld on the back of my cart.

Like always, I felt myself relax as I stared into the cool blue water, lapping occasionally at my shoes. The bottom of the pool was lost in whatever chemicals they pumped in to keep it that lovely shade, and I liked that. I could imagine falling forever, in a bottomless blue expanse. A place where they couldn't chase your rent or dock your pay because you were two minutes late. Where you were unknown, anonymous, free.

The blue had held me throughout those fourteen years. I hadn't had a favourite colour before I'd gone in. I'd thought that stuff was for kids. Ellie – Eleanor had one back then of course. I figured that question now would get me a shrug and a yawn, if she were in a good mood.

The rain trickled down the glass, falling away down the muddy hill on the other side of the windows looking onto the pool. The brown shade of clogged toilets and smug screws. I looked back at the blue.

There had been a window in my cell. A simple rectangle of toughened glass behind a lattice of steel bars. It got dirty in the winter. Sometimes people cleaned it from the outside. Sometimes not.

But in the summers, I used to stretch out on my bed and watch that little portrait of blue deepen in colour as the day wore on. Not thinking about anything, not feeling anything.

Imagining what it would be like to reach out and touch it. Feel it on my tongue. It was the one spark of colour in that place.

I'd had a phone in there. I'd had to trade all my fags and my first sloppy blowjob for it. It was small, one of those old Nokias that could survive an H-bomb. Luckily for me. I'd had to hide the fucking thing up my arse for a decade. I was sad to leave it behind when I left. It knew me more intimately than my ex-wife had, before Stephen and his five Rembrandts in a row.

It got me through the winters. I'd take a picture on a shining July afternoon, when I knew the screws were screwing elsewhere. Every year, I'd make sure I got a different one. I hung a piece of dark cloth over the window when the season turned and pretended it wasn't there. Then I'd shit out my phone at 2 a.m. and look. And dream.

I'd painted the walls of the flat blue on the day I moved in. It helped with the yawning expanse of the bathroom, the auditorium of the living room. I worried sometimes that the space would eat me up. The blue helped with that. It helped with everything.

I looked down at the pool as I finished up, the water seeming to call out to me. I wondered what Baxter would think if I stepped in, fully clothed, and let it wash over me. I could probably get a full thirty seconds before he came barrelling down the stairs on his little legs and sent me back to Derek with a sore backside. No matter. I was content to look.

The kid's pool only took half as long. Baxter remarked on my report sheet that I did a much better job with the adult pool, and suggested I do it last to avoid "slackness", underlined in red. But he didn't see the echoes in there. The life rafts that might have been, the grinning inflatable tigers that never were, the rings decorated like sugared doughnuts.

Maybe I'd buy her a pack on the way home. Stephen was a harsh task master. Scrambled egg on wholemeal toast every morning, and a glass full of pureed kale. It wasn't saving his hairline or doing anything for Eleanor's imagination. I'd just about choked it down on that morning he'd had me over, for a "man-to-man" after Nicole had gone to work. I considered that day a testament to how well I could swallow bullshit.

I left the centre as the first families began to arrive, still in my uniform. A little girl was holding a young mother and father by the index fingers of each hand, the fire of life in her eyes. I smiled at her, but she didn't see me. I didn't look at the parents in case it hurt.

My car sat in the forbidden car park. It was blue too, an ancient Corsa I'd bought with my first few payslips. Inside it, I felt at peace. Harmless. Free. The rest of the day was mine to do with as I saw fit. Whatever that meant. Eleanor was free to come over after school, if she wanted. She just had to text me, and I'd pick her up. As long as I asked Stephen first, naturally.

I drove aimlessly for a while, before the sky made me anxious again. Then I headed home.

I lived over a kebab shop now, and therefore never wanted to eat kebab again. I pulled into my parking space and looked inside. Lunchtime, and the place was bustling. People laughing, dripping grease onto complementary copies of The Sun. They scared me too. I wanted to get upstairs and look at the walls.

I was about to go when my phone buzzed again. I considered leaving it. Probably Derek again, asking how my day was, with another fucking smiley face. But I had to appease the man. At least until the man found a tastier fish.

My heart stuttered as I read the message. I hadn't saved the contact. Typing out the name hurt me. And Stephen had given me the number. But I knew it, as well as I knew that slice of blue sky. Eleanor wasn't a wordy girl. They said she was better at maths. The text simply read: "u there".

And suddenly, in that blue car, under a grey sky, fourteen years later, I was there. I was finally there. I reached out, fingers shaking on the face of the phone, and told her so.

MINISKIRTS & REVELATIONS
by Margaret Graham

(NODA award for excellence 2014)

In this funny and moving play, baby boomer Penny returns to her childhood home, looks through her teenage diaries and takes us back to the 1960s.

The main characters are the Greenfield family – three generations of women: Grandma, Mother, and teenage daughter Penny. The theme is the different roles women play throughout their lives and their quests for fulfilment. This is a time for rethinking commitments and expectations as waves of disturbing post-war revolutions in politics, morality, fashion and music affect the whole of society.

How will Grandma's Victorian values cope with this? Can Mum find fulfilment in her domestic role running the family's guesthouse? Can Penny's downward spiral into ever-shorter skirts and tartiness be curbed? Will biker brother Mick remember to wear his skid-lid?
Most intriguing of all – why is Grandma not what she appears to be?
And will the Health Inspector ever dare to touch her gravy?

'Incorporates touches of tragedy, mystery and humour ... A most entertaining play.'
Phillip Hall, NODA Area Representative

An Extract:

SCENE 7

PRESENT DAY PENNY:
For someone born before the twentieth century had dawned Grandma was surprisingly open minded when it came to some things - fashion for example. And yet, looking back, it was strangely at odds with the Victorian values that her parents must have drilled into her. Take this diary entry of mine for instance: 'Friday morning. Woke up feeling awful. Tec Open Day. Feel better now I'm dressed in my new gear. I look fab! Grandma agrees. Just had an interesting chat. ...'
I remember that chat ... and the terrible event that followed.

Lights come up on the guesthouse kitchen. Grandma (in her floral pinny) enters and starts preparing elevenses

Music: What's New Pussycat – Tom Jones

Penny enters from the back stairs wearing a minidress, high white boots, a floppy-brimmed hat and carrying a bag. She walks and twirls around to the music as if on a catwalk.

PENNY It's from Biba, Kensington. What d'ya think Grandma?
GRANDMA I like the colour. Where are you off to in that?
PENNY The Tec
GRANDMA Tec? What's a tec when it's a home?
PENNY Technical College. Open Day. To look at the courses on offer. All the sixth form are going. Boys too. (*Pause*) Dad wants me to do a commercial course – shorthand and typing.
GRANDMA And what do you want?

PENNY Pitman's course is boring. I want to be creative. You know, drama or dance maybe.
What d'ya think? *(Dances)*
GRANDMA Dance? Like on TV? The Go-Jos? Top of the Pops stuff?
PENNY Yeah. Oh, there's a thought. Singing! *(Puts a record on the player)*

Music: Shout – Lulu

PENNY *(miming and dancing)* … then I could dance AND wear super clothes I've designed myself. With your help Grandma. *(Hugs her. Turns the music off).*
GRANDMA Elevenses dear?

Penny nods and carries the tray of tea things out to the kitchen doorstep/patio. They settle themselves - Grandma on the bench, Penny on the doorstep as usual.

GRANDMA It's time you understood something dear. When we're grown up, as you nearly are, we can't always choose for ourselves. Got to keep our feet on the ground. You should think about that typing course. It's very sensible. And I might not always be here to help you.
PENNY I can't believe it Grandma! You always stick up for me, even against Mum! And look at Mum – she always does the sensible thing – running our guesthouse all by herself – except for you Grandma, of course. Dad away all the time. She might as well be an unmarried mother!
GRANDMA Penny!
PENNY Dad's miserable all week 'cos he wants to be home with us and he's stuck in a boring, disappointing job.

GRANDMA It's his duty to support the family. Someone has to pay the bills. Money for all your outfits doesn't grow on trees you know.

PENNY And Mum. What does she ever do that's exciting or creative? Something that inspires other people? Do you think I want to be like them? If that's duty you can all think again!

(Penny sulks. Grandma pours Penny some tea, taps her on the shoulder and a reconciling smile passes between them as Penny accepts the proffered mug.)

GRANDMA (*thoughtfully*) Your dress is a lovely cut dear. But it's very short. If you bend over in that everyone will see your stocking tops and suspenders. I'm not sure that's a very … fab … look.

PENNY That's alright Grandma. I've got some tights.

GRANDMA Tights … tight … What are tights?

PENNY These are tights Grandma. (*Pulls some out of her bag and hands them over*) I carry spare ones, they're very fine, ladder easily, see?

(Grandma inspects them closely.)

GRANDMA Two stocking legs joined to knickers. All in one. That's an American invention, I'll be bound … Even got a gusset … Mmm … (*Looks at the gusset, then at Penny*) …
But there's no ventilation, dear …

The phone starts ringing …

DEAD ORDINARY
by Judy Apps

Whether I should tell you about Art before his wife died or afterwards? Afterwards, certainly, he showed surprising courage – considering the man he was before, I mean. A man who never answered the door, but let his wife deal with tradesmen, neighbours or family, while he lurked in the garage, tinkering away under the car or filing a key which didn't quite fit, happy to saunter in later, not showing surprise if there were visitors but not as if he expected them either. Certainly, any comment he made wouldn't refer to their arrival, but to what he'd just been doing, "I could fix that carburettor if only I had the right tool ..."

Afterwards? Well, afterwards, if he was going to stay in the same house and that was never in question, then he had to step into roles he'd shied away from in the past. And he did that. He kept the house spick and span. He cooked. He did well, for a man of eighty. He went further and joined an industrial archaeology club where, shy as he was, he could talk widgets with like-minded people. But the surprise to his family came the day he remarked in passing, "I plucked up courage and joined a sculpture course at the Adult Education yesterday."

His children, Nancy and Tom, knew all about their father's enthusiasm for new "projects". There'd been the year he converted the old air-raid shelter into a wine store, the creation of a sunken garden with pond, the installation of a dark room, and much else. But none was as intense as this.

Nancy visited one afternoon and found him poring over plans. "It's my design for a kiln," he said to her enquiring look. "It'll record the exact temperature at each stage of firing. I can build the main part with fire bricks. I just need to source Kanthal wire to make the heating element. There's a place near Brighton that sells thin sheet aluminium for the door, so I'll drive down there on Friday ..." Nancy's attention floated away on his familiar technical talk.

Art went regularly to the modelling class, parking his car at the centre at least half an hour before his session to 'set up' ready for sculpting that week's nude model. He grilled the tutor with detailed questions every week and was soon known as a "character". He made accurate body measurements to get the proportions correct. His creations became larger until they no longer fit his kiln, and against advice he began firing them in pieces and fixing them together carefully afterwards.

Within a year, he was bored. "Everyone works too small; but large clay models get too heavy and unstable," he complained. He joined a course on casting and invested in chemicals and resins. Over weeks and months, he cast a life-sized dog, a Great Dane, for his dog-owning son. Tom wasn't sure where to put such an outsize gift, eventually opting for a spot outside by the back door.

Art was now ready for his magnum opus – a dancer in resin who would stand poised in arabesque, arms stretched out high and wide. He intended to place it at the top of the garden, visible as soon as visitors came in the gate.

~~~

One July morning, Nancy opened the gate into the empty garden. Funny how a garden loses its soul when its owner is gone. She remembered when he was alive, how she'd cross the grass to find him on his favourite bench, and he'd suit his rustic setting somehow, with his rope-like arms and face full of life's wrinkles. But without him, it was just overgrowth and neglect. Shabby really.

There was the dancer, cleverly balanced just as intended, dominating the lawn. She gazed at it. Impressive. Almost wonderful. She remembered him describing his plan for a dancer leaping in jubilation. But it wasn't balletic, nor graceful really. She wondered what would happen to it. Who in the family would have room for a life-size model, now that he was no longer around?

The sculpture encapsulated her sadness, that her father had spent so much effort on a sculpting project that almost worked. Story of his life, really. Earlier clay sculptures placed around the garden were already crumbling, damaged by lawn mower knocks and destructive winter frosts. Towards the end, when his brain couldn't work out the complications of resins anymore, he quietly gave it up. His last sculpture – a kneeling dancer - languished in the little workroom next to the kitchen, too current to abandon, but too abandoned to continue.

~~~

Leaving the lawn, she strolled over to the well. It was 40-foot-deep, and the cover had been another of Art's projects, everything hand-made, even the metal supports hammered into the brick sides, the cover itself an old door hand-sawn into a circle, suspended a foot below the header course of bricks. He was a scrupulous worker to be sure, but she had never trusted it enough to let the children anywhere near when they were small: too scary.

His silent joke was still there – in terrible taste, but funny too. At some time, Art had moulded and fired various hands of clay, cut off at the wrist. Hands are notoriously difficult to sculpt, and he'd put in quite a bit of practice. He'd placed a few of them wrist side down on the wooden well cover, so that it looked as if the hands were straining to get out of the well. Amusing and horrible. She shook off the feeling. Well, she wouldn't be the one to clear them away; this was just a quick visit to say goodbye to the place. After months of illness, accidents, hospitals, his final days, she was dog-tired; ready to move on. She circled the house, past the back door, past the vine she'd given her father one birthday years ago, now setting grapes for another bumper year. As if it were just one more time and not the last, she walked firmly out of the back gate, got into her little Skoda and drove away.

~~~

Today, I'm back. I always take the main road now, and never turn down the lane that passes my dad's house. I don't much like to travel that road anymore. But today a road diversion sent me this way. It shook me up somehow. His house has gone. The buyers assured us that they loved its history, but in the end, they pulled it down and started from scratch. Only five years, but different times. Life goes on after the death of parents. We feel like orphans for a while, then adjust to our new position in the family tree. Yet every now and then small triggers have the power to disturb shadowy corners of memory. Treacherous history refuses to stay fixed in the light of who we are today and has a tendency to throw up new insights in disturbing waves of feeling.

I've been thinking a lot about my dad recently. We weren't hugged much as children. When I was in my twenties, I used to notice school kids embracing and kissing and wonder what it would feel like to be so comfortable in your body. I sometimes think my dad hung onto his projects to avoid all that, and I wonder why. What moulded him? Was he just a man of his time, or was it something else? I now love body movement – yoga, Aikido, tai chi, Five Rhythms – there's something amazing about someone in tune with their body. Recently, I've been watching the daily practice of a Five Rhythms teacher on YouTube. Feeling unsettled after my trip past the house today, I sank onto the sofa on arriving home and switched to one of these Five Rhythms videos. The dancer started slow, uncertain almost, and then built in stages, gradually increasing power and intensity. I was caught up in his movements as they became freer and larger, until he approached the climax and threw his arms high in the air, expressing sheer ecstasy with the freedom of his body, thrusting almost beyond his reach: shoulders, arms, palms, fingers all stretching in the thrill of the moment, oh, that, that!

I lunged forward and stopped the video. I couldn't breathe. There, there was the image, there was the feeling. Not a balletic arabesque, not grace, not flow. The hands aren't balletic, not at all. They are stretched to their utmost, fingers apart, crazy almost, with the huge overwhelming power of joy. That was what Art was after, an exalted abiding statement, "Here. Is. Joy!"

You knew that feeling, Dad, you knew. All those hands you sculpted in efforts to capture that awesome sensation, to greet everyone that entered your garden with joy. And I never knew that you knew: I drowned in your widgets. I'm dizzy with the knowledge, sad as well, and so, so proud of your noble endeavour. How extraordinary, to seek to capture a feeling so awe-inspiring, to greet every visitor into your domain with a welcome of joy!

Tonight, I lie in my bed and walk in dream up to the old house, struggling a little at first with the rusty gate. Then I enter the garden. There you are, sitting on your favourite bench. And there's the statue, your ecstatic welcome. Your yes to life! My heart fills with the generosity of that, and my face breaks into a smile.

LOE BAR, CORNWALL
by Diana Barclay

With gentle breeze and sun enough to warm,
This piece of nature's universe stands still, untouched,
untorn.
Keen eyes my own, do gaze upon a large compelling lake,
It flows in gentle peacefulness to dream and never wake.
Birds meet in swarms to play upon its massive face,
Then shadow glide to seek its cool embrace.
Its watery depth gives home to countless mass,
Of weeds in many hues and forms, of fish fan-tailed and
brash.
A universe complete within its well,
Where life amidst its life feels free to dwell.
Love revolving Love.

BRIEF SIDE, CORNWALL
by Diana Barclay

In solitary mood I stumbled on my haven,
It was staged in wonder, dressed in radiant gold,
A winding path weaved webs amid the cliff tops,
While angry torrents swelled with pride then rolled.

With anxious eyes I searched for the horizon,
Turquoise rose to kiss with softest blue,
I heard the crying echoes from the boatmen,
Shrill screams from hungry seagulls as they flew.

Grasses wild grew full in buoyant fashion
To amble at its leisure where it please,
Aspiring high to weave majestic music
To complement the whispering of the breeze.

I did not ever want to leave my haven.
So wistfully I sat and lingered there,
The gold had turned to silver of the evening,
Deep clouds of purple laced the quiet air.

I brushed aside the grasses of my mountain
And sought to recognise the well-worn lane,
Replenished by this visual show of beauty,
I joined the breeze to hum its sweet refrain.

POSTERITY – CHAPTER 1
by Jess Newton

(To be published by Gurt Dog Press in Winter 2021)

Captain Nina Brooke blinked as the haze lifted and everything started to come back into focus. Warm air rushed over her, soothing away the chill lingering in her fingers and toes. The face of her Chief Medical Officer pixelated into clarity, dark curls framing her serious face, then her words started to register.

"Welcome back, Captain. Remember to take it slowly."

Nina eased herself into a sitting position and rubbed her eyes, chasing the last shadows from them. Dr Caimile backed up slightly to give her room as she stretched and looked around her. The cryobay looked exactly as she remembered it, enormous and sterile. It felt like no time had elapsed since she lay down in her pod.

"Whew. Any idea how long we've been out?"

"Not yet," the doctor replied, shaking her head. "I've been awake five minutes longer than you; I just had long enough to run checks on myself before I got the alert that you were waking up. Now, if you don't mind…" She gestured to the medical unit in the wall and Nina got down from the table that had been her cryopod, crossing gingerly to the recess and stepping in. She felt the familiar tingling sensations as the unit assessed her but ignored them, focusing instead on running through her next tasks in her head. After years of preparation, it was about to begin. The thought gave her a pleasant adrenaline rush as she tuned out the physical. After a moment, the unit bleeped and a small receptacle containing a number of pills emerged from the wall next to her. She threw them back and stepped down, grimacing as she swallowed them.

"Alright, Doc. Prepare to wake the rest of the crew. I'm heading up to the bridge to check it's not a false alarm. I'll let you know when we're good to go."

"Aye, Captain. Try not to overdo it."

The ship was eerily quiet as she walked the hallways to the bridge, and she wondered again how much time had passed. It seemed like only a few weeks ago she had been supervising the final checks on the Posterity and readying it for this journey, but providing there hadn't been a malfunction and they were indeed nearing their final destination, that had been over fifty years ago now. How much had changed, back on Earth? Assuming there still was an Earth, of course.

Chiding herself, she firmly pushed away the bleak thought and concentrated on the here and now. She reached the doors to the bridge and swiped her hand over the access sensor, letting it read the chip embedded there. The doors opened and lights sprung on, illuminating the large, empty room and the sleek control consoles spaced evenly around it. She made straight for her chair in the centre of the room and checked the date and their position, flicking the toggle to hail Dr Caimile down in the cryobay when she had finished.

"Brooke to Caimile, are you there?"

"I'm here, Captain. Go ahead."

"It's not a false alarm. We're right where we should be, about a week away from our new home. I'd like you to start waking the crew. I'm going to stay up here and read up on what's been happening a bit more, but call me back down before they're awake, I want to be there."

"Understood, Captain. Caimile out."

Nina skimmed through the mission briefing on her console, reminding herself what was next on the agenda. They'd have a week before they arrived at the planet to check through everything more thoroughly and there were people on her team with specialities that made them more suited to the job than her, so she contented herself with scanning the list instead of absorbing it. After less time than she thought possible, Dr Caimile's voice rang through the empty bridge.

"Caimile to Brooke. You've got about five minutes until the crew start to wake up, Captain, I'd recommend you get down here."

She pushed herself to her feet, flicking the toggle to reply as she did so. "On my way, Doctor."

Caimile greeted her with a nod as she walked back through the door of the cryobay; a huge, hangar-like room right in the belly of the ship, with rows upon rows of units stretching off into the distance. Those set to wake up first, like her, the Doctor and the rest of her crew, were positioned at the front of the lines, nearest the door. The rest of the colonists were carefully arranged in groups, their cryopods on tracks for ease of movement, ready for waking when their time came.

"I've staggered them slightly, so I can get them all into the med unit in turn. Liu is first."

Nina crossed to the table she was indicating and saw her First Officer going through the last stages of waking from the enforced sleep. She stood back as Caimile stepped forwards, enough to be out of her way but still obviously visible should Liu look for her. She could tell the moment he woke fully from the way his whole body tensed, even before his eyes snapped open.

"Are you all going to do this?" the doctor asked, exasperated, as she pressed firmly down on the man's shoulders to stop him from sitting up too fast. "Lie back down, you need to take it slowly."

Nina let out an amused snort. "We are soldiers," she pointed out. "At ease, Liu," she added, raising her voice so the still prone man could hear her. "There's no rush." His eyes found hers and he relaxed as he took in her casual stance. After a moment, Caimile released him and he sat up slowly, swinging his legs over the edge. He looked smaller than she remembered, having spent fifty years unable to look after the muscles he had worked so hard to maintain before going to sleep. Liu was relatively short, but made up for what he viewed as a deficiency by looking after himself meticulously and keeping himself in prime physical and mental condition. Nina had known him for years and trusted him implicitly, both on and off duty. He grinned up at her and she smiled back, more relieved than she cared to admit to have him awake again.

"How're we doing, Captain?" he asked, rotating his wrists in front of him.

"All according to plan so far," she returned. "Now go get in the med unit, I'll debrief everyone together." He nodded and hopped off the table and she turned her attention to the next pod.

They went through the same drill seven more times until the rest of the team had been woken and checked over. Things progressed without a hiccup until Ramin Chaudhary, the Quartermaster, woke up, and exclaimed loudly that he couldn't move his legs. The newly woken Nurse Taylor, a young, attractive, black American man, came rushing to his side in a panic, only to see Chaudhary grinning broadly as he pulled himself into a sitting position.

"That wasn't funny," reprimanded Dr Caimile, as she helped Chaudhary into his wheelchair. "He's only just woken up himself, he could have done serious damage rushing over here."

"Sorry, Nurse," Chaudhary said sheepishly. "But it was too good an opportunity to pass up."

"What do you bet he planned that one even before he went to sleep?" Caimile muttered aside to Nina, as a still uncertain Taylor accompanied Chaudhary to the med unit.

"Oh, without a doubt."

When everyone was finally awake, the medical assessments were done and the doctor had pronounced everyone fit for duty, Nina stood proudly in front of her crew. The mission was a global effort, so Nina had been lucky enough to take her pick of the people she wanted from all over the world. They were all specialists, experts in their field and chosen with care to form a cohesive team and avoid clashes in personality. They looked ready for action, smartly dressed in their military uniforms; grey jumpsuits with the orange logo of the United Earth Space Force embroidered on the top left pocket, black undershirts and black boots. They were all slightly paler and thinner than they had been, but otherwise unchanged. She smiled at them and took a breath.

"Welcome back, everyone. It's been fifty-three years since we left Earth, and we're a week away from our destination. So far it seems everything has gone according to plan. The ship's log has recorded the release of all the planned communications satellites, and we've been getting regular updates from Earth. Kjeldsen, I'd like you to take a look over those please." The Communications Officer, a tall, young Dane with blond hair and dark eyes, nodded. Nina turned her gaze to her chief engineer, an elegant Russian woman with a knack for machinery she'd never seen matched in anyone else. "Pavluhkin, I'd like you to check the status of the ship. We're arriving in a week, which means if there's anything that needs fixing, we need to do it now. Everyone else, stick to normal routine until we know what we're dealing with. Liu, with me. Dismissed." The crew saluted and left the cryobay, leaving Nina and Liu alone amongst the sleepers.

"How're you feeling, Dan?"

Liu grinned at her. "Surprisingly ok thanks. How about you?"

"A bit achy, but alright. I want you to keep a close eye on everyone in the next few days. I'm sure the doctor will be doing so as well, but it might just take everyone a while to adjust to the fact that so much time has passed and I don't want anyone to slip through the cracks."

"Of course, Captain," Liu nodded his agreement. "It is kind of weird to think of everyone back home being older, isn't it?"

"That's exactly the kind of thing I mean. Some people may deal with that knowledge better than others and I don't want anyone suffering in silence."

"I suppose it depends on what they left behind," Liu mused, his eyes roving over the endless lines of cryounits. Nina squeezed his shoulder in sympathy; she knew that Liu himself had nobody in particular to regret leaving, following the recent death of his father, but that in itself was a form of regret. Nina had no family left either; both parents had passed away years ago and she had been an only child. The military had been her family for a long time now.

"Come on, let's get to the bridge and start going through it."

All the other bridge stations were occupied when they reached it a few moments later and Nina slipped into her chair as the pilot, a young Maori woman in her twenties named Samantha Fraser, announced the customary 'Captain on the bridge' from her position at the helm.

"Carry on," she responded, waving her hand in a gesture of dismissal. She loaded up the document listing the protocols on preparing for arrival at their destination and absorbed herself in that, making sure she was as familiar as she could be with what was to come. She lost track of time until a gentle cough jolted her out of her work and she noticed Kjeldsen, the Communications Officer, in front of her. "Yes, what is it?" The young blond fidgeted and Nina, looking closer, saw that they looked noticeably distressed. "Alright, let's take this somewhere else," she said, standing. "Liu, you have the bridge." She gestured for Kjeldsen to precede her towards the doors, then ushered them into the small meeting room adjacent. "Ok Kjeldsen, I'm listening. What's up?"

"It's Earth, ma'am."

Nina took a sharp intake of breath, cursing herself for not reading the reports from Earth earlier when she had the chance. "What's happened to it?"

Kjeldsen shook their head, tears shining in their eyes. "It's in a bad way, ma'am. I've gone through all the communications from Earth, and to start with they were as expected. They hung on for about ten years after we left. But after that, the entries are different. Both polar ice caps have completely melted and ninety percent of the previous landmass is now underwater. There have been riots, uprisings, coups; even wars. There were some big nuclear blasts when people started placing the blame. They estimate the remaining population is around ten million people."

"Christ," Nina exhaled, turning away. "Did they manage to get any more ships off?"

Kjeldsen nodded, but their face remained grave. "Ten. The situation escalated too quickly for any more to be organised. We can expect two here, one in thirty years, one in twenty-five. From what I've gathered, they've been sent with a lot less equipment than we have, too. They just didn't have the preparation time."

"We don't need to worry about that yet," Nina said firmly. "We'll bear it in mind, certainly, but if we've got twenty-five years before they arrive that's more than enough time to get this planet up and running first." She sighed. "I'm sorry you had to go through all that. If I'd known, I'd have tried to spare you."

Kjeldsen squared their shoulders and looked her in the eye. "With all due respect, Captain, it's my job."

Nina nodded, impressed by Kjeldsen's professionalism. She didn't know much about the young Dane; she had worked with them on one previous mission and remembered them as being calm, capable and in control, but this was beyond what they had dealt with in that job. Christ, it was more than any of them had ever dealt with.

"You're right. Would you please make me up a report that I can deliver to the rest of the crew? I'd like them to hear it from me."

"Of course, Captain. I'll get right on it."

She nodded and they saluted, leaving her alone in the dingy grey room. When she heard the doors close behind them, she sagged, finding the back of the nearest chair and leaning on it for support. Ten million people left on a planet that had held billions. Ten thousand more on each colony ship, of which there were now fifteen. She struggled for a moment, unable to comprehend the destruction of her race on such a large scale and grateful for the chance to deal with the information in private before she had to present a brave face to her crew. She remained a few minutes longer in the meeting room, composing herself before returning to the bridge. Liu met her eye with a worried gaze and she shook her head.

"Not yet."

He turned aside, knowing her better than to push her before she was ready, and she attempted to return her attention to her preparations. Two hours before the day's shift was due to finish, Kjeldsen handed Nina their report. She read it thoroughly, impressed with the concise nature of their work and feeling more prepared to break to the news to the crew.

Due to the automated nature of the ship, it wasn't necessary to keep a watch at all times so the crew ate together in the mess. It was Monique Leclerc, the Chief Science Officer's turn to cook first, and the galley buzzed with energy as the crew chatted, getting to know each other and praising Leclerc for her culinary prowess. Leclerc was a round brunette with a razor-sharp mind and she had prepared a simple pasta dish with the same attention to detail that she gave her work.

"I'm afraid I have some bad news," Nina announced after the plates had been cleared. She stood, walking up to the head of the table so she could watch their reactions as she delivered Kjeldsen's report. One by one, their faces fell and she watched as they cycled through shock, denial, anger and too many other emotions to name. She gave them a moment to process the information before she straightened her shoulders and continued.

"This news only serves to strengthen the purpose we have here. Our mission to this planet is now more important than ever. We hold a wide range of people in our ship and our job now is to give humans a new home, one we can continue to develop the best of humanity on. When we arrive, we begin again, and this time, we build to last. Humanity will go on and we are the ones who will make it so."

Liu raised his glass. "Hear hear."

There was a murmur of agreement from around the table as everyone imitated him. Tears shone in more than one pair of eyes but the atmosphere around the table had changed, and the crew had gone from defeated to determined.

"Let's call it a night, then, and I'll see you all in the morning." Nina nodded at the table in general, making eye contact with a few people and striding swiftly from the room. She knew they'd want to discuss the news she'd just imparted and Kjeldsen would be glad of the opportunity to recount the information too. It was better for everyone if she left them to get on with it while she went and got some sleep while she could.

PAINT ME A PICTURE
by Pauline Watson

Once I too
Painted those pointless flowers,
dipping brush, captured as seen
each petal, leaf, copied for hours
reproducing their silken sheen.
But now I
Lay vast canvasses
across the studio floor
colours without restraint
swing paint on strings
from vaulted ceilings.
And then I
Ride bicycle tracks
splatter paint smacks.
Did I mention, "Art for Art's sake?"
That scrambled mess I make
I know it is out of fashion
art made with such passion.
Then she said
"Galleries won't stock it,
There's too much 'shock' in it,
random dashes, painted slashes,
slapdash colour that always clashes.
Dramatic texture is far too 60's
paints you mixed, simply missed it.
Try pastel pale circles, couldn't be worse,
Why don't you imitate Damien Hirst?"
Let me be

Forget the greys, go Hollywood Pink,
indigo, here we go, Ferrari red
sunshiny yellow, chocolate spread
colour me scarlet, dots and dashes,
more violent, vivid measle rashes.
But now
Life is not all gloom and doom
an email has arrived, out of the blue
amazing, someone wants to
buy the lot, for a millionaire.
But he just
Wants information to send money, where?
 pass all my bank data for him to share
passwords, and my codes? An email
to transfer money, I check the detail.
Sadly then
Respond by saying, "email received. No thanks,
my money stays much safer in the banks!"
And so
meanwhile, in a corner of the studio
more stacked canvases will have to go
until my peacocked genius is seen
that will be as far as they have been.

THE EXTRACTION
by Pauline Watson

The dentist held his probe
"It has to come out," he said.
Mask shimmered in the strobe
waved the needle nearer my head
"Just an injection, maybe two.
Numbs the site. Should do."
He turned to his waiting nurse
words followed of course.
"Just lie back for a while."
His teeth made a smile
gleaming and sparkly white
like stars that shine in the night.
Ten minutes, he lifted the probe
stabbed me once in the mouth
scrabbled around going South
"Quite numb, didn't feel that?"
It was numb. It wasn't that
the glimpse of the pliers
drowned out my cries
and he pulled, and he pushed
crunched and crushed
cracking and racking
sounded like fracking
as bit by bit, my tooth came out.
"All done." He said, still fishing about

A great wad of cotton wool
I stood, wobbly as a foal,
Then the bill was enough
To make me feel rough
And into the car park
Home in the winter dark.
My face is swollen and sore
I won't eat toffees no more.

PULSE
by Rosie Basten

Full bodies glisten -
We prepare our sanguine homes
And cautiously, listen
As fingers twitch for pulse of thread
To know we're not alone.

Interconnected,
Reclused but not rejected -
Our silk once slick with envy
Comes pure with beads of gold.

Truths now told:
We've nothing to do
But -
All eyes open,
Nest into our well-spun webs
And reel the light and hope in.

YUGEN
by Rosie Basten

A pebble glistens
In the nape of the sea:
Touched by water
Touched by light
I grieve with a thousand colours.

WILL AND I
by Nicholas Mackey

When I was young, I spent some time with Will Shakespeare and it turned out to be an unforgettable experience. Will was just so wonderful to have around. Then one night, disaster struck, and we were separated when a river breached its banks. I was caught up in the ensuing deluge and nearly came a cropper. Fortunately, I was rescued, and Will and I got back together. You may have noticed I'm on first name terms with the nation's foremost figure in drama and poetry. All that was during my tender years or, as I like to call it, my misbegotten youth.

Oh sorry, let me explain. You see, by chance, we found ourselves as freshly-saved and occupying our own two places in Reed's Literary Emporium, a bookshop of repute 'at the sign of Queen Boudicea', but with a difference near Bankside, London. The saved bit of this story will become clearer in a moment but I'm happy to say in the next few months, Will and I became well acquainted and built up a wide circle of friends from the learned realm we came to call home: a labyrinthine premises full to brimming with all manner of books, pamphlets, large heavy tomes, maps, posters and sheet music spilling on to the floor such was the multitude of items for sale. By special royal warrant, Reed's was also authorised to sell the Holy Bible and there was no shortage of parishioners in need of its hallowed words of divine guidance. In addition, The People's Register, a daily newspaper was proving to be a popular item with all copies sold by the noon bell of the minster of Saint Saviour and Saint Mary Overy on our doorstep in Southwark.

From my vantage point, upright beside Will, I was able to peer out the window and frittered away the interminable mornings and afternoons watching the world pass by this emporium. I also spied many a person who ventured inside bearing a vexed countenance and became so absorbed in their reading that hours could gently pass before their departure with a face relieved of their tribulations, and sometimes a smile would touch their lips.

For us inhabitants of this fascinating corner of London, we looked forward with glee when the last customer had gone for the day. The owner, a Mr Ralph Reed, a man of noble disposition, would lock the front door and depart at the tolling of six bells from our local church inviting the faithful to Evensong. That was when our fun began inside this theatre of passion shelved and longing for a life lived. We could let our hair down, shaking off our servitude of stillness and exchange anecdotes repeatedly in stitches at Will's spot-on mimicry about the comedy of goings-on throughout the day. His astute comments about the pomposity and folly of countless patrons of Reed's were such an eye-opener. Ye gods, how he kept us entertained which helped I must say alleviate the tedium of being left on the shelf, as it were. In my case, I suffered countless strangers touching me, taking me in their hands, opening me with abandon and running their fingers all over me so that I felt debased. And dirty. To add to my despair, the persistent pain of rejection I can never forget, which left a scar I'm sure when hastily replaced with a sigh beside my bound brothers and sisters. Many's the time I pondered on how they survived.

But there was another, shall we say, earthy aspect to where we were located in this vast metropolis and it definitely introduced a frisson of excitement to our lives. This tempo in our routine continued with some of our members moving on and new companions making an appearance until a wretched flood wrought havoc with all of us back in 1598; I recall it well as it was a decade after the Spanish Armada.

How did all this come about? A bit odd really as a collection of Will's plays and I were brought into this world as separate entities by Cresswells, the stationers in Marshalsea by the debtors' prison on the southern reaches of old father Thames. This gentle lad called James was our maker, a 15½-year old apprentice who put us together with care and great application though Will and I were saddened to be cast aside so early on when the merchant who had ordered us went bankrupt so I found out and didn't take delivery. The master printer, a Mister Kit Cresswell, was a callous man and we were consigned to a limbo existence as a forgotten heap of cast-off publications on the floor of this busy premises. People would trample o'er us and I felt the painful step of countless shoes press into my spine but James had made me robust so I was able to bounce back; Will too was of equal strength. We lay there close together, Will and I in this unseemly manner for ages until a white-haired and distinguished-looking gentleman materialised one day. For the first time someone took an interest in this library of downtrodden souls and our good Samaritan was the very same Mr Reed who kindly took us out of this god-forsaken hole by purchasing us as a job lot for his Emporium on Gropec*nt Lane in the aforesaid Bankside nearby.

I have to say the next chapter of my adolescence turned out to be anything but boring for a variety of reasons. For starters, the bookshop as our new abode was prone to flooding from the adjacent Thames which time and again disgorged its putrid contents into the surrounding area and once I was fished out from the inundated basement a sodden, grubby wreck in danger of falling asunder. The proprietor must have relished his profession because the pragmatic Mr Reed, who supplemented his income from the business of literature by running a bawdy house on the uppermost two floors of his establishment, cleaned me up and dried me out executing his deed of love so well the term 'river soiled' no further applied. But I have an inkling you might be interested in what else occurred at this location. Permit me then to satisfy your prurient curiosity.

As a resident in a building dedicated to the printed word on the same site underneath the uncouth bawdy house or more commonly called a house of ill repute in today's prim manner of speaking, I became familiar with so much thanks to Mr Reed's Little Bit of Paradise. It swiftly became a popular establishment albeit with a certain notoriety where gentlemen from all positions of society found comfort in the women my new guv'nor employed.

Often, I beheld an excited punter satisfying his lust with a whore from the Paradise above – and once in a while more than one strumpet partook – between the shelves when the upstairs rooms must have been fully occupied. I have to say my education all through this period was of the raucous and thrilling type. My early years after coming into being were exhilarating as I learnt plenty of stuff from events and people that were not recorded on the written page. A lot of know-how, some of it of the forbidden variety, I picked up by simple observation. Little by little, I taught myself how to see and keep my ears open with a modicum of intelligence, if I can say such a daft thing about myself but I had to laugh at the irony of this place which had become my home, where holy writ and unholy shit were both available under the same roof.

With resignation, I accepted the lesser status in our relationship and admired my dear Will's ability in his writing to rise above us mere mortals as we eked out our base lives. It seemed as if Will was like a star soaring beyond the cosmos unchecked by the petty needs of subsistence carving out a dazzling pathway for himself but there was I, a minor actor from one of his tragedies who falls prey to some dire setback: I was 'fortune's fool' and knew it. The luck of the proverbial had smiled on him, as Will had escaped this terrible flood that almost destroyed Mr Reed's bookshop just about taking me with it; I narrowly escaped a 'muddy death'. Providence, nonetheless, took a hand yet again and, after my rescue, by coincidence Will and I ended up back on the same shelf together side-by-side after repair work had been carried out and the Emporium re-opened to lavish fanfare.

In the meantime, the brothel trade had continued to flourish with clients a plenty crossing the threshold in search of instant gratification which Mr Reed's sordid kind of Paradise on earth provided for a fee but there was a lingering odour about the setting: was it the residual dampness mixed with the dirt from the recent unwanted attention of the filthy river or was it perchance something else?

You see, something niggled. O muse of my inner self please grant me forgiveness as I hesitated in delivering my well-rehearsed rebuke to Will and my group of friends who, in spite of being well-read and of an intelligent character, were oblivious of the harlots' lot. I shall never forget the sound of tormented weeping of one young woman languishing in her indignity within this bookish cube of inner space late of an evening after the departure of her in-and-out lovers and their wanton ways. Didn't those pals of mine not hear those same tears of shame and disgust? I can still feel this mighty guilt of mine emerge from depths previously foreign to me 'cos I bit my tongue and did not speak out. I was a coward. Why must momentary human pleasures be rooted in such lingering pain? Why is it so?

Will was entirely unscathed, however, by all these mucky goings-on, the jammy devil. I envied him his favourable aura, his way with words and how his finely bound edition with gold leaf lettering was so frequently handled with such fondness and read with fervour by those yearning to delight in his genius. I ask you, they even tried to nick Will on several occasions but fortunately for the bookseller the ne'er do wells were always apprehended and the stolen goods returned. The miscreants were most fortunate not to suffer the gibbet at Tyburn but Mr Reed, in true Christian spirit, forgave his wrongdoers. How many times I heard people laugh and occasionally weep at what my chum Will had written down. When recited with feeling, his language seemed to be possessed of some magical metre that bore his followers to another enchanted universe. Ye had to hand it to Will and his way with words. His rhythm reigned supreme.

But as for me, I was seldom chosen and invariably out of error but more commonly as a sense of duty or as a means of assuaging guilt from the decadence of luxuriant living as I felt my solemn temperament could be a killjoy and I can remember some readers groaning in despair when they read me. How I ached for the same sentiments of affection Will was continually in receipt of. In truth, I was envious, nay jealous of his popularity and the only reason Will lay on the shelf beside me for so long was that he was a special commemorative version costing an exorbitant five shillings and seven pence farthing, the equivalent of the annual earnings of the apprentice who had given birth to him on the Surrey bank of the river a while back. On the other hand, I was a cheap print run of a tome preaching the hallowed merits of the avoidance of evil and temptation. Huh, from what I have experienced so far in my brief span on this unholy earth, is that the good is oft-intertwined with the bad. But I've come to the realisation that because of my sanctimonious tone, no thief had ever tried to steal me. This is a stinging regret.

But as I've come to understand, wealth will have its way and one bright summer morn, a well-dressed woman, unusually bareheaded, but blessed with exquisite black hair and bewitching brown eyes entered the premises with a flourish followed by her chaperone, a demure lady of mature years, presumably a maid of the bedchamber. Our distinguished young visitor was an heiress I figured on account of the quality and vivid nature of her attire who could not have been more than one and twenty and the sunlight momentarily danced upon the most subtle of pearl ear rings she wore. A dainty lace handkerchief poked out from her left sleeve which I am sure was perfumed as she held it close to her face. This personage of note announced in a sweet voice to our proprietor that she was buying on behalf of her father, Sir John Radford, she said for the regeneration of an old library in Oxford University which had an unusual name, the Bodleian, I believe.

Mr Reed fell under the spell of this doe-eyed temptress and a purchase of books was agreed after considerable haggling and I ended up on my travels again. But I experienced the nearest thing to ecstasy when the young Lady Radford – I regret to this day I never did catch her Christian name – carelessly gathered Will, myself with some other neighbouring volumes and held them in a handful next to her sweet-formed bosom exposed somewhat as a button on her bodice had come askew. For a few fleeting seconds, I was pressed against her right breast and I rejoiced when a delicious flowery scent mixed with the fragrance from her soft glowing skin enveloped me before she handed us over to be wrapped in crinkly brown paper and bound up with old twine. I savoured this short-lived but intimate contact with such a handsome lass and it compensated for all the disappointment in playing second fiddle to my comrade in arms, Will. I must say though I didn't fancy the insect that leapt from my mistress Radford's clothing and which lodged itself in my binding. I fear it might have been a pregnant flea as she gave birth within me after an interval and I became alarmed with tiny creatures let loose within my delicate folds but mercifully – and may the good Lord spare me for such a wicked notion –when these mites perished soon afterwards I was thankful. In time, their decayed bodies then became part of me.

In my short life on this earth so far, I felt I had been witness to so much but now a famous town of learning beckoned – a seat of scholarship and intellectual endeavours where books would be treasured as I was hearing about. That was something to behold and filled my fledgling heart with such joy, if such a thing is possible in me as a mere whippersnapper of a mass of words printed carefully in sequence on my bound pages.

Oxford: from the titbits of information, I'd discovered about this idyll, there was something in the sound of this place that was a clarion call to adventure, my years ahead filled with promise. Goodness knows where this fresh optimism sprang from, but I sensed it pulsing up and down my spine and, a general air of happiness was palpable in this library of the silent.

It was the day of departure and I tingled all over on this sun-filled morning as we trotted along the highway, called the Great Worcester Road I had gotten wind of from the conversation I'd eavesdropped on earlier. We were heading out of London in some sort of horse-drawn contraption guided by a ruddy-faced, rotund man of middle age who must have been fond of the hard stuff judging by his intemperate diction and unsteady handling of the two unfortunate nags pulling on the reins. I had understood from the vulgar exchanges between our coachman, if you could call him that, and an ostler in the yard behind Reed's Literary Emporium and A Little Bit of Paradise where copious drink was taken during a convivial breakfast, our itinerary had been chosen and Oxford was to be our destination later this day. It was also agreed the venerable Sir John and his lovely daughter would be journeying separately in a few days but no doubt in more comfortable circumstances than us mere books piled into a rickety old cart open to the elements. I prayed the skies would remain becalmed and it wouldn't rain. Another drenching would be the end of me, I'm sure.

As we pushed on with our passage westwards through this frenetic mass of people pressed together in this great city, I could hear the hustle and bustle of London about me, above me and beside me and the air carried an array of fragrant aromas of bread and the preparation of food from nearby bakeries, hostelries and other establishments. To my surprise, the scent from some seasonal flowers that somehow had managed to conquer this urban sprawl to spring forth with such dazzling hues. Unfortunately, I was unable to avoid the unwelcome stench from the open sewers running down the centre of many streets and also the various streams, creeks and rivers which serve as foul-smelling cesspits on the move, some tanning factories and slaughter houses and the odd privy we passed by. I hoped we would make it safely despite the errant concentration of our so-called coach driver under the influence and the pot-holed King's thoroughfare not to mention the vagabonds and thieves who might have lain in wait for us enroute.

I glanced about me and took in my fellow voyagers in print, all of us gathered together as a motley collection of stout-backed, separate small repositories of language designed to entertain, guide, scold, inform, shock and all manner of things the written word can do to us rocking to and fro in unison as we travelled on. But sadly, I was without my excellent and witty friend, Will and his dramatic prose by my side as we'd become separated again somehow but on this occasion for keeps, I feared. How grateful I was though I had had an opportunity to share such a special bond with Will Shakespeare, a unique individual if ever there was one albeit for a brief time.

Our driver cracked the whip and we gathered pace on what seemed to be a smooth stretch of road that skirted some woodland. I noticed a number of trees with their green-laden branches swaying in response to a mild breeze which played out a serene symphony: a melody of leaves rustling one against the other and I was in awe of the miraculous tidings about me beneath a blue and cloudless sky arched so high and far away.

It looked as if we were leaving the metropolitan melée behind and open countryside began to embrace us. I spotted a sign indicating the village of Hammersmith as a bird came into view. I wished now I had paid more heed to that illustrated almanack on the flora and fauna of the earth which shared the shelf with me in the book-filled Emporium but I reckoned it was a swallow on account of its forked tail and a distinctive red patch on its chin. I marvelled at its ability to set a winged course within the ether as it soared into the firmament in front of us. The miserable environs of Gropec*nt Lane and Bankside were now luckily out of sight.

I found I was buoyed up by the wondrous weather, the cherished memories of an unorthodox start on this earth in our grand capital in close proximity to a glittering interpreter of the written word, the delight of exploration and gaining knowledge from the unexpected. I pondered on how charmed fortune had moved the hand of a beautiful damsel to select me in the company of others to be part of some grand collection within this great Bodleian Library. I had guessed she was a maiden on account of the absence of a band of gold on the fourth finger of her left hand.

I gave thanks for my deliverance and wondered, "When will I see this attractive woman again and what on earth is her name?"

I may be nothing more than a slim, imperfect volume entitled, The Path Onwards And Upwards extolling the virtues of 'a wholesome way of life' (whatever that means) but even I can sense the thrill of anticipation and a brand new will to live as I depart for a new existence in Oxford. I am in seventh heaven. My future shall be unlike the past, no longer will I be a cork floating on the surface of some waterway addled with putrefaction but instead I am resolved at being in command of my fate. Methinks I have the makings of a bold heart and a sound mind as I summon up the strength, I knew not I possessed.

With Will's distinctive dulcet tones echoing from within as we proceeded on our way, yet another question vied for my consideration,

"Am I up to my destiny?"

Authors note: This is a work of escapist fiction. The role played by Shakespeare in this narrative is entirely fictional. Events, locations/establishments cited, all other characters mentioned and also the publications, 'The People's Register' and 'The Path Ahead' are fictional. London, Tyburn, Bankside, Bodleian, Thames, Hammersmith and Marshalsea are real however but their representation here is part of this imaginary landscape. Any resemblances are purely coincidental. By the way, London did once possess several Gropec*nt Lanes.

THE EVE OF AUTUMN
by Sally-Claire Fadelle

Yesterday it changed
My neck and my knees
Felt it first,
I searched for another layer
In melancholy mood
For Summer
Was leaving

Breath of the breeze
No longer warm
Chill gaining edges
My shoulders shudder
I sniff in whispers of changing seasons
Shifting slowly,
Gaining pace with each dewy dawn
Sun now veiled in grey
Allowing little warmth
Even when bright

My basket holds
The first signs of Autumn
The humble ingredients
For soup.
Not flirty
And flamboyant as the mixed salad
Oozing Spring,
Offering Summer's promises
Tempting colours

Vibrant
Bright
First in shades of green
Of gold
Then rainbow strands and leaves
Of ruby, yellow; red and orange...
But the solid
Satisfying roots
Food to be trusted
Offering no flimsy Summer romantic notions...

... a truth,
Earthy potatoes
And knobbly swede,
Turnips, celeriac, sprout tops
And winter greens
Imagined in a hot broth
Slurped in big jumpers
With oversized necks
Reaching down
To meet sock tops
Curled in a chair

Steamy windows
Crying for those
On the wrong side
Without a home
Often alone
With no big jumpers
Hoping for soup.

THE DARK SIDE OF THE HILL
by Lena Walton

From the Journals of Layla Lawton
(Read out in the trial of October 25th, 2020)

On first meeting, Troy had the appearance of a down-on-his-luck eccentric. Sometimes his dress bordered on tramp. Throughout the summer and the early autumn, he was always in shorts and a T-shirt. Some days it was obvious that the same clothes had been worn too many days in a row. He was painfully skinny; not a part of his body had a layer of fat. Yet he was not physically fragile, there was a sinewy strength to his body that suggested something alive and strong. He had the look of someone who needed a woman to look after him, to care for him. Working out in all weathers as a builder, he had a leathery, wind-harassed face. Sometimes bearded and sometimes clean shaved; as if suddenly remembering his appearance was important, if not to him, to someone else.

However, his speech suggested something entirely different. He was well educated, erudite and sharp witted. A sharpness that could cut you down in a few words. Dangerous; a dangerous kind of wit. It was something that I could not reconcile with his outward demeanour, the eccentric tramp and the cruel narrator. Two sides to his character; the clothes that gave the impression of kindness and the words that gave the impression of a cruel manipulator.

Chapter 1 – Troy Buckley

When Troy first set eyes on Layla at the bus stop that summer morning, he was fascinated by her. She was almost ethereal; not of this world. Not really living in the real world, that was for sure. She seemed untainted by all the trappings of society. But she was also the most unapproachable woman he had ever encountered.

And it was then, as he looked at her, that something cruel and feral roused itself in him. He wanted to bring her down to the dirt; to smash her, to destroy her, to make her just like all the other women he had encountered.

"Faint heart never won fair maiden."

Never truer a saying was that on that first morning he encountered her. She barely spoke to him, just raising her head from the book she was sitting reading. Later he saw that book on her kitchen work surface and remembered the title and the front page, 'The Terror', with the depiction of a cold artic landscape and ice trapping a ship.

At the time, he didn't give it a second thought. Of course, she would hide her head in books because she certainly didn't seem good at making conversation. What surprised him at that first meeting was how she affected him.

Troy was down on his luck. He was desperately in need of a daft, single woman who was living on her own. Someone whose life he could smarm his way into and ensure that he was in a warm, comfortable place for winter. Someone he could manipulate, mess with their head and control.

He could see that Layla was not that woman. She had a coldness about her but also a strength that he thought could, and ultimately would, defeat him. She was not the easy way out and yet he wanted her. It was such a powerful need in him, greater than his need for alcohol. The demon that ruled his life suddenly changed to something of a more curvaceous and sensual form.

So, the next morning he walked to the bus stop, thinking about her. Maybe she is married, maybe she is in a relationship. But her aloofness suggested that no, she would never demean herself to be cohabiting with a man. Up until now, he mused. Troy was suddenly up to this challenge. He would bring her down.

Disappointingly, that morning she was not at the bus stop. He had figured that she would be catching the same bus at the same time every day. He then remembered the neighbour who sometimes gave him a lift; perhaps she had stopped and given Layla a lift that morning.

He concluded that there would be other days and other opportunities. He was in no rush. However, he would like to have his feet under some lonely lady's table before winter set in on the hill.

The next day she was there. And she said hello before he even prompted her with his, "Good morning, Leah." Then he saw her face twist in annoyance and heard her say, "My name is not Leah. It's Layla." And then she promptly stuck her nose back in her book, making it obvious that any chance of a conversation with her was now not going to happen. He sat down on the bench next to her in silence, feeling like a naughty schoolboy.

But he just couldn't leave it there. He had set her in his sights and the game would not end until he had caught her.

A few days went past and he managed to have several conversations with her. Each one made him want her more. The way she spoke, her vocabulary, the serious look on her face. The way her thick, wavy, dark hair tumbled around her face. Those deep, almond-shaped, dark eyes, flitting from anger to a look almost questioning everything around her. Her slightly swarthy complexion suggested to him that she was not English or that perhaps her family were not English.

And he had moments, when he looked at her, that he thought he knew her from somewhere. But where, he could not place. He felt sure that if they had met before he would have remembered. Most of the women he associated with were stupid, Layla definitely was not. Perhaps it was just that he had passed her in the road in the village and up to now had not been fully aware of her.

Then suddenly his circumstances changed, he no longer needed to catch the bus. He moved home. Still in the village but no longer with the chance of seeing her. He was now being given a lift to work and didn't go past the bus stop where she waited each morning. Likewise, she too was suddenly conspicuous by her absence.
When Troy started to ask about Layla, it surprised him to find that very few people knew anything about her. For a woman that had lived up on the hill for over 15 years she was almost a mystery. Those that did know of her merely said, "Keeps

herself to herself." "Works long hours." "Think she may be from the Middle East." "She plays that Arab music sometimes." "Can be a bit snotty."

None of these comments surprised him, especially the last one. But even a lone wolf has a thirst for company. She must have some kind of social life, he thought.

He had hoped she would be in their local pub at the weekend. Saturday, he went in for a drink as usual and she wasn't there. Again, when he enquired about her to Curtis, the manager, the question was met with a blank. "Not sure who you are talking about, mate. It doesn't sound like any one that comes in here."

Maurice, the local womaniser, said she had been seen in there once or twice but that was it. Of course, it would be Maurice that had spotted her; however reclusive she was he would have noticed her on her rare appearances.

Then finally one Saturday, as June was burning into an equally hot July, he got on the bus to go down into town for the morning and she was sitting there with her nose in a book, as usual. She looked up and acknowledged him.

He saw that her skin was now a honey-roasted colour and then he remembered the last conversation they had. How had he forgotten? She was going to Beirut. Hence her being more elusive than usual. She had been away. Why Beirut? He had asked himself when she had first mentioned it. Strange place for a holiday. But then he didn't even have a passport, so holiday destinations were not something he often thought about.

He stared at her for a moment. The sun had only improved her in his eyes. Even her eyes seemed livelier, less angry than they had been before her holiday. She seemed ever so slightly more approachable, if that was possible.

Knowing that he only had this opportunity to move things forward, he glanced at her hands to double check that there was no wedding or engagement ring. Then he asked, just to make doubly sure she was not with anybody, "Are you single?"

The reply in retrospect was not surprising. "Yes I am. No one would have me. I am very difficult to live with, apparently." Her voice was dripping with irony. Troy wanted to laugh. She really was a cold one.

Undaunted by her reply he continued, "How are you with meals?"

"Oh, I am house trained." Again, with that same tone and a rather arrogant look on her face. The need to slap it away came across him but he remained impassive.

"Do you fancy a meal in the local one night?" He was expecting a sneer of derision, but instead he got the reply, "Yes, why not?"

Troy hoped he contained his pleasure at this response. Nevertheless, back on form, when they discussed what night to meet, she replied with, "How about next Saturday?"

A week, she was making him wait for a week. Just what on earth was this socially inept and reclusive woman going to be doing each evening for the next week?

He had scored a goal. But something in his head said, this is too easy, Troy. Way too easy.

He got off in town and watched the bus, with Layla still on it, drive away. Where was she going? Perhaps, she does have a life, maybe friends. Stranger things have happened in this world.

His plan had been to go and see Debbie, a casual, very casual ex-partner. Her husband was meant to be out of town at a football match up in Manchester. Suddenly he couldn't be bothered. She was not really of any use to him. And now that he had someone far better in his sights, he needed to be, to all intense and purposes, single.

He didn't bother ringing Debbie. He just did his shopping and got the next bus back home. By the early afternoon, and a bottle of Vodka later, he was in a stupor; oblivious to anyone and anything.

Chapter 2 – The Uncovering of Skeletons

Kristina was at a bell ringing rehearsal in the local church in preparation for Saturday. She was tugging at the ropes in a rather half-hearted manner with her thoughts being elsewhere. There was a new man in the village and he had all but ignored her. What was she doing wrong?

To be fair, she wasn't that interested in him. Yet the fact he quite clearly wasn't interested in her bothered her. Why wasn't he running around like a puppy? Tongue lolling out of his mouth, panting and generally looking forlorn.

Was her age becoming an issue? Too much Botox? Not enough Botox? Was her assisted blonde hair not assisted enough?

No way, she reassured herself. She was still the sexiest woman in the village. As far as she could establish, he was single; a single male not making a play for her. Just what was going on?

She had asked a few questions about him, but it was all a bit vague. He had been living in one of the caravans up at Hill Crest but then had suddenly moved in with Joseph, one of the other resident recluses. That was a surprise in itself. Why had Joseph agreed to that? Everyone knew he was reluctant to have anyone living with him since the last lodger had left owing him three months' rent. And the two before that had committed suicide.

Local gossip, which Kristina did not involve herself with, said the place was cursed or haunted. Or perhaps it was Joseph. Maybe he was hell to live with. But he seemed to be just a recluse who went in the pub for a drink and then went home. Anyway, he had decided Troy could stay with him for whatever reason.

Was Troy in a relationship with someone else? Perhaps he was having a break from his wife. The space meant to give them time to think. Kristina knew that meant normally the husband having a fling with someone else then eventually returning to the wife, the wife none the wiser. Kristina knew only too well about the theory behind having a break, space to think. She had bedded enough of those men in that space. There certainly was no thinking going on there.

Suddenly her focus switched to that woman that lived up at Hill Crest – Layla. Another person the villagers knew very little about. Another social recluse and she had lived up on the hill for 15 years.

Kristina had tried to make friends with her when she first arrived. Her first offer of, "Would you like to help with our charity fund raising event for a new roof on the church?" was met with a reasonable rebuttal.

"Thank you for asking, but I work really long hours, so would not really be of much help."

When Kristina had asked around her circle of friends about Layla, they had all seemed in agreement about her. "Social recluse." "Works long hours." "From the Middle East." "Plays that Arabic music." "Can be a bit snotty."

Undeterred Kristina continued to try and make friends with her. The next time she saw her on the road, walking, she attempted a conversation on a culinary theme. "We are holding a village meal in the hall. We would very much like you to come along. Perhaps contribute with some of your Arabic cooking?"

There had been a look on Layla's face that suggested disdain. Again, she had seemed to have a genuine reason for not being able to attend. "Sorry Kristina, I will be away in Syria for a few weeks."

If Kristina had been a suspicious sort, perhaps she may have noticed the trips to the Middle East that Layla seemed to embark on frequently. Kristina wasn't a suspicious person.

The other thing she wasn't was a gossip. She had too frequently been on the receiving end of that in the village.

When the rumour mill started going around about this woman being a member of ISIS, she just dismissed it all as utter nonsense. There was any number of reasons she was hiding up there but ISIS was not one of them.

Kristina was stopped in her deep thoughts by the vicar speaking to the small group of campanologists. "And that's it for today. Thank you, as always, for your dedication. Saturday, let the bells ring out loud and clear for Sandra and Martin."

Kristina stared at the vicar as if she had suddenly remembered who he was. The replacement for the last vicar. The one she had an affair with, that had almost ruined her marriage and brought down the Church of England.

The young man, Brian, had been swiftly despatched to a new parish and his replacement, Nigel, was suitably old and frosty so as not to be another distraction to Kristina.

As the small group were leaving the Church to walk back to their respective homes, Doris began to chatter inanely. "They have found a body up on the hill, another body. That's at least three," she said with conviction.

"Two. Actually," Chloe corrected.

Doris was one of the worst gossipers in the village. More so because she never even came close to the truth. Most gossip needs an element of truth to it and Doris just didn't seem to have any of the facts with her stories whatsoever.

She had gossiped about everyone in the village, yet barely knew any of them. Even their names were a blur. Her latest subject was a corker.

She had managed to spread the news that the body recently found up on the top of Box Hill was the remains of Mr Tugwell, an 80-year-old man who had succumbed to cancer in a nursing home in Eastbourne.
Instead of such an inconspicuous demise, Doris had decided a gang of Hell's Angels bikers, who regularly met at Ryker's car park at the bottom of the hill, had killed him. It was part of a particularly vicious killing spree on one of their usual Sunday morning meets.

Kristina had tried to explain that it was not possible. How the hell had the poor old sod even managed to get himself down the hill let alone piss the local Hell's Angels off enough to kill him? And everyone saw him being taken away in an ambulance with his very tearful youngest daughter in tow, following the ambulance in her very new BMW.

The gossip at the time had been more about how she had been able to afford the car before her dad was even dead. Especially as by then number 12 Hill Crest was in complete disarray and falling into the ground. In fact, the shed seemed a better place to live than the actual property itself.

Then, of course, there was the ensuing battle between the members of the family that meant they couldn't agree how to sort out the property. No one in the family seemed to want to live in it, so they sold it back to the landowner and then suddenly the mysterious Layla was in there living the life of the enigmatic social recluse.

It came as no surprise to hear from Doris that already three bodies had been found on the hill. By the end, it would be 50 or maybe 100. All killed off by leather-clad bikers on their Harley Davidsons, fuelled by sex, drugs and rock 'n roll. If only they would just drop by her place, just once, Kristina mused.

A CORNISH ADVENTURE IN NOVEMBER
by Jill Benson

I went to St Ives for a week at the end of October and stayed on for five weeks on my own, making it up as I went along. On my return, I discovered that my house had been broken into by the police. But that is another story...

Here are some extracts from my diary.

DAY ONE

Late start this afternoon after a good lunch, so only a tiny walk along the cliffs from Geevor Tin Mine to Boscwallen Cliff. How can I call myself a walker?!

Cauldron of sea, churning, spewing, at the foot of the cliff. Only a swell - by Cornish standards - but spectacular, nonetheless. Dusk picked out a silhouette of engine houses and chimneys and various other ruined outbuildings, pools and ditches. Remnants of Cornwall's tin mining past which haunt the coastline. In the half-light they looked like the remains of an ancient civilisation, and I suppose they are, really - certainly something from another age. If I squint, the pillars that are left could almost be Roman. (To paraphrase the great Reggie Perrin, "we wouldn't be where we are today without them...".)

Impressive sunset-sky coated with layers of fluorescent 'jam', red leaching from the tear in the sky, like a wound.

As the light was fading fast, I met a woman from Suffolk - now of Pendeen - walking her funny, shaggy, yappy little dog. Cautioned me (as all women do) about the dangers of walking on my own, 'especially at this time of the day!'. I said I liked being 'at one with the earth' and she replied with a smile, "Being with my dog is enough for me!' I tried to convince her to give it a go, but she wasn't having any of it.

Oh dear, I am benighted! At least I've got off the - by now rather hazardous - cliff path and stand a fighting chance of finding the car. Haven't done a night walk for ages, but is *so* dark in Cornwall and eerily quiet. After all, I'm a Surrey girl, and it's only this quiet back home at 3.30 in the morning when the deathwatch beetle comes out. (Apparently, this beetle was thus named because people often die at this time of the morning.) So - moving on....

The West Cornish version of 'quiet' is so thick it wraps itself around you in a comforting sort of a way. All I can hear is cows munching, a noise which seems to have been strangely magnified in the silence - perhaps they are giant cows, of a type only found in this part of Cornwall. Even I have been 'magnified' - my silhouette is of a giant, apparently towering over the stone wall. Perhaps it will scare away the 'giant' cows...

Later, the sound of the wind and the sea crashing onto the shore is punctuated by a strange wailing sound from the Pendeen lighthouse. I am amazed how loud the sea is, even half a mile away. I love the way that life in Cornwall is so governed and shaped by the weather. In the mornings, back at my B & B, one of the first things you hear on local radio is the weather/shipping forecast.

Coming from landlocked Surrey, I get the impression the Cornish are much more in touch with the elements than we'll ever be in the south east. Many of them have told me they love living here and will never move. I think much of this is to do with the unique landscape and the more relaxed lifestyle it fosters.

DAY TWO

On the way back from Penzance, stopped off at the Coldstreamers pub in the tiny village of Gulval for a three-courses-for-the-price-of-two deal. As it's the low season, there are bargains to be had, if you're prepared to search them out.

I came across this pub by chance, having remembered the unusual name. Connected to the Coldstream Guards and, according to the visitors' book, many soldiers have stopped by. Recommended to me by a girl I met in a pub in Penzance, who used to work for the owner. The Coldstreamers is run by two brothers from the village and has a great menu. Feasted on mussels, hake and an ice cream trio. Delicious.

Loud, shouty, young girls talk loudly about their new iPhones, the price of property, work and their next holiday. Why do they need to make a private conversation so public?

Interesting, off-beat man from the Basque country, with unusual spectacles, served me. (Myopics, like myself, notice these kind of things.) Spoke to him in French and - eventually

- asked whether he was a Basque Separatist. Replied he'd 'separated' by coming to Cornwall 10 years ago. When I changed tables to get away from the awful shouty women, he asked whether I'd be changing tables for each course. I said I hadn't decided yet.

Basque man admired my dog-eared OS map and my French accent. He had also walked the coast path, but hadn't bothered to take a map. 'Not like the Pyrenees', he said, 'where you're done for if you can't read a map'.

This man doesn't do niceties - 'I won't ask you how it was - I can see', he announced, as he removed my plate of empty shells. Lives in Penzance with his baby daughter, and says he has only one friend, who was born in the house where the Penlee Art Gallery now stands. I rather got the impression that if his girlfriend hadn't become pregnant, he would have returned to Spain. Was he sad and resigned or just being ironic?

Nicer here in this old-fashioned, cosy pub with a roaring fire than being alone in the B & B. Although my tiny two-bunk ante-room with TV is adequate (in fact, I have two rooms), it gets a bit lonely in the evenings. At least it's straightforward driving home tonight back to St Ives. Some nights I get quite lost, which is very tiring, as I'm chief tour operator, driver and walks/events organiser.

Returned late to Hilltop B & B and grabbed one of the boiled sweets Jan always leaves out in a dish on the sideboard.

Popped in to say goodnight and Jan told me there is now a Frenchman staying upstairs. He never comes down for breakfast or, apparently, leaves his room. Also, he refuses to speak French. In fact, he hardly speaks at all - in any language. Stays in bed until about 5pm each day. Tom - Jan's husband - says he's heard him shouting. Jan doesn't mind as long as he's paid (which he has - in advance). We are wondering whether: a) he's assembling an arsenal of weapons upstairs; b) is cutting up a dead body; or c) has someone else up there.

Option no. 3, according to Jan, is not uncommon. She is the most flexible landlady I have ever come across. I've already been here three weeks and she's never asked me for a penny. Unusual. How refreshing.

Another room has been taken for three weeks by a lady Jan calls 'the Jill substitute' ('only Jill hasn't left yet!'). The latter has become a well-worn theme, as each day at breakfast when she asks me if I'm staying on, I reply 'just another night'. In fact, I've been nicknamed 'Just Another Night Jill'. Mmm, could be taken the wrong way...

Anyway, the 'Jill substitute' is also staying for longer than the average B & B guest, and is an elegant, pretty, young Indian girl, who works as a physiotherapist. Friendly, a smoker, and the girlfriend of a local chef. Jan thinks she's rather exotic and Tom said, 'Bit of a looker!' Jan looked over her specs at him, sniffed and went up to bed.

I stayed up watching telly in my little TV room and, sucking a boiled sweet, watched a ridiculous C4 programme called 'Dirtiest Homes in Britain Two'. How glad I am I don't have to do the cleaning when I get up in the morning! I wonder what tomorrow will hold??

HARVEY'S GRIN
by Alison Allen

'Not again, Millie? That's the third thing this week.' Mum fingered the rip in Millie's school bag. 'What's going on?'

Millie didn't answer. If she told Mum about Ethan, the new boy, she'd have to explain everything. She cuddled Harvey, their golden retriever, playing with his floppy ears. Harvey wriggled happily, giving her his special grin. It was their secret code. 'Let's play, Harvey,' she said, waving his favourite half-chewed tennis ball. Maybe Mum would forget about the bag by tomorrow.

The next morning Millie pushed her cereal away. 'I'm not hungry.'

'You need to eat something,' Mum said, whisking dirty breakfast dishes into the sink.

'I don't feel good.'

Mum's damp fingers touched her forehead. 'There's no fever,' she said. 'You'll be fine once you're there.'

Ethan was lurking by the school gate when Millie arrived. She hung back, waiting for him to go inside. The playground was crowded with other kids, but Ethan was on his own as usual. In spite of everything, she couldn't help feeling sorry for him. Having no friends was horrible.

In the classroom, Miss Morley had re-organised all the seating. Ethan was on a table by himself. Millie was squeezed between bossy Laura and her best friend Jessie.

'This is my space,' said Laura, spreading her arms in a large triangle across the table. She leaned over Millie. 'That bit's Jessie's.'

Millie curled herself into the tiny space that was left and tried to get on with her number work. It was hard to think against Laura's chatter. She sneaked a look at Ethan. He didn't seem so big when he was sitting down. Or scary. In fact, stuck on his own when everyone else was working together, he looked...sad.

At lunch, Millie made her food last until all the other kids had gone and smiley Mrs Carter started wiping down the tables. 'Hurry up or you'll miss your chance to play outdoors,' she said. Millie said nothing. Playtime was no fun without friends.

That afternoon Miss Morley said they could do some painting. Laura, spreading newspaper over the table, shut Millie out altogether. 'You can share with him,' she said, pointing to Ethan.

Ethan did not look up when Millie timidly put down her paper. He was drawing a picture of a dog. Relaxing, she started mixing blue and green paint, ready to paint her favourite mermaids. The table wobbled violently. 'Stupid thing!' Ethan yelled, rubbing furiously at his picture.

'Don't!' Millie said, before she could stop herself.

He scowled. 'Stupid thing. The leg's all wrong.' He tried again. Then he flung down the pencil and scrunched up the paper.

'What are you doing?' Millie asked.

Ethan grabbed the jam jar of water and threw it over her mermaids. 'Think you're so clever? Let's see them swim.'

Millie froze. Her masterpiece disappeared in a swirl of dirty water. Ethan reared up, toppling his chair. With an angry shout, he swept paints, brushes and paper onto the floor.

Miss Morley looked at the dripping water, the mess on the floor and Millie, speechless in the middle.

'Outside,' she told Ethan.

Ethan did not return to class that day. At home time, Miss Morley held Millie back. 'I'm sorry about your painting,' she said. 'I'll make sure Ethan apologises tomorrow.' She tucked her hair behind her ear. 'He's having a difficult time. I'm sure you understand what it's like, starting a new school...'

Millie nodded. She still got a lump in her throat if she thought about her old friends.

'You're a kind girl, Millie,' Miss Morley said. 'I know you'll be patient.'

Being patient wasn't enough. Two days later, Millie was picking her way round the playground where the boys were playing football when there was a shout. Something hard smashed into her, bowling her over. Then she was on the ground, bits of gravel digging into her cheek. Above her, Laura was telling the teacher, 'It was Ethan, Miss. He pushed her.'

Millie stayed at home the next day. Dad worked on his laptop while she watched films. By the time afternoon sun was streaming through the windows, she was bored.

'Can we go out somewhere?' she asked.

'Sorry, love, got to take a call,' Dad said. 'But you could go to the shop and get us some beans for dinner. Take Harvey, he needs a walk.'

Outside, afternoon school was over. The streets were busy. Millie took the short cut back through the park.

She was almost home when she saw Ethan. Her heart pounded. 'Run, Harvey,' she urged. The lead tightened as Harvey leapt forward, yanking her arm. Her feet slid from beneath her. She felt herself falling.

An arm reached out and pulled her up. 'You dropped this.' It was Ethan, holding the can of beans.

She grabbed it and backed away, gripping Harvey's collar.

'I'm sorry about yesterday,' Ethan said. 'It was an accident. I wasn't looking.'

Millie stared. Was he telling the truth? With Harvey beside her, she felt brave. 'What about the other stuff?' she demanded.

Ethan kicked the grass. 'I know. I'm sorry. I just get so mad sometimes.'

'That doesn't make it ok for you to keep picking on me,' said Millie. 'Come on, Harvey, let's go.'

Harvey did not move.

'I have a dog,' Ethan said, kneeling down. Harvey licked his face. 'I mean, I did. Then my parents split. When we moved here, Mum said there was no room for her….' His voice wobbled.

'Did you have to give her away?' Millie asked.

Ethan nodded.

Harvey rolled over to be tickled. How would it feel, Millie wondered, if Harvey wasn't there? Frowning, she watched Ethan playing with Harvey's floppy ears. She couldn't believe it when Harvey broke into his special grin.

When Ethan picked up the old tennis ball, Harvey sat up, quivering with excitement. Ethan sent the ball spinning into the air and they sprinted away together. Millie watched through narrowed eyes.

At last, Harvey returned to flop at her feet. Ethan jogged back, his face flushed with happiness. He looked like a different boy. 'I'd better go,' he said. 'See you at school tomorrow.'

Like an old friend. A friend who loved dogs as much as she did.

Millie did some quick thinking. 'You can help me take Harvey for a walk, if you want,' she offered.

Ethan's face lit up. 'Really?'

Millie handed him the lead. 'Really,' she said.

And as she looked down at Harvey, she could see he was grinning.

TARGETS
by Richard Howard

Exuberant on his stolen moped, Ryan spotted his target, revved the engine and mounted the pavement, scattering screaming pedestrians in all directions. The young woman unable to tear her attention away from her phone, shrieked with outrage and shock as it was snatched from her hand and the rider disappeared, weaving his way dangerously through the traffic. It was the work of an instant.

Back with his gang, Ryan was the hero they all envied as he brandished the trophy for which he already had a buyer in mind. Inspired by his latest feat, two of the gang immediately sped off to do the same, or something even better. Competition was rife as they all tried to out-perform each other.

That afternoon, Ryan ditched the moped, smashing it in the process, and set off to find another. If you knew where to look it was easy to locate some rich kid's pride and joy left unattended and insecure. He'd stolen four in the past three months and never used the same one more than a few times. That way he'd never been identified and never encountered the police.

The police were worse than useless, too afraid to pursue a moped once the rider removed his helmet in case he was injured or killed in the pursuit, resulting in the police being prosecuted. Government cutbacks meant fewer police on the streets, political correctness tied the hands of those few, and

Ryan's gang became the scourge of the city, modern-day highwaymen in all but name.

With police resources stretched to breaking point and disillusioned officers leaving in droves, Government targets played straight into the hands of the gang who made rich pickings from anyone they had in their sights. Easy targets were tourists, inattentive and unfamiliar with their surroundings, and of course, the legion of addicted young men and women unable to tear their gaze from their phones in the street.

But phones were relatively easy to grab and as competition in the gang intensified, some returned with briefcases, laptops, handbags and even designer watches, anything that challenged the skills of the rider. These blatant thefts regularly hit the headlines, another source of pride for Ryan and his gang. They laughed at the ease with which they could snatch a bag when the target walked too close to the edge of the pavement, unaware of any danger.

The police, still at a loss, had other things to focus on, not least the threat of bombers who despised the way of life led in the country that had given them refuge. They were the enemy within, a higher priority than tearaways on mopeds who knew this only too well. With common sense and basic caution, they could get away with anything. Not one of Ryan's gang had ever been interviewed by the police about moped theft or anything else.

They congregated in parks or back streets, always changing their rendezvous to avoid attention. At the end of every day, they met in high spirits to share their stories, to show off their spoils, and to gloat at their stupid victims and the pathetic police. They celebrated the latest headlines, criticising authorities and urging increased public awareness. The same edition reported the latest bomb threat that was consuming all police resources, useful information for the gang, making them feel invincible as they mocked and jeered, determined to take advantage of this distraction. The following day was a field day as every member of the twelve-strong gang turned out to cause mayhem on the streets and boast about their exploits.

Meanwhile, all police attention was focused on a suspect who had been under surveillance for weeks. This was the day they made their move. Tracking him on street cameras, they seized and arrested their target. During interviews, the suspect repeatedly protested his innocence. The backpack he'd been wearing yielded nothing suspicious. But where was the bag he'd been carrying in his hand? Just as the question was asked, a blinding explosion elsewhere in the city sent commuters rushing for cover as they passed by the central park where a group of youths had just gathered.

A dozen named victims of the tragedy were listed and mourned next day in the evening press, all young men with, as the report put it, 'their whole lives still ahead of them'. But for once, there were no reported incidents of street theft.

THE MOON AND MEMORY: ILLUMINATIONS
by A A Marcoff

the moon have I seen in that land faraway, a moon that shone like the mind: the moon have I seen in that land faraway, a moon that shone like the stars: and I was living in the old part of Tokyo, sleeping on the matted ground: sleeping in a six-mat room, on tatami, that is so simple – humbling and ordinary and beautiful...

and I remember, I remember that time, one evening in September when the land was autumnal, how they drove us from the school in a number of cars through Tokyo suburbs, to a Buddhist temple that was hundreds of years old, where the old wooden architecture curved into the mind: I remember how we all sat, all of us teachers, out on the verandah, in rows that were perhaps four or five deep, how we faced the night sky and the clouds: and the clouds passed like ages of history: and the priests chanted their prayers, and beat small drums, and intoned holy names, and we sat in silence to view the autumn moon in a tsukimi, or moon-viewing ceremony: and the moon was full and white like a poem: and the brief beauty of the full moon now, most beautiful at this time of year, was our celebration of Mono no aware, the beauty and transience of things, the way beauty comes and goes, is fleeting, and how we can in the words of Blake kiss 'the joy as it flies', and so touch eternity...

and after a period of silence and contemplation, tea was served to us all, with some pink globular sweets, and these were the symbols of the moon itself, which we were going to eat, as in a dreaming: the old temple was our theatre, our ancient site or circumstance, that yet held the moment of the present, immediate, illuminating: I drank the tea, as if it were the essence of moonlight, the fragrance of time passing, and the silence now of that haunting night: and I am certain that this moon still shines to me now, a light in the poetry of my being, a light that bathes old stones in the grounds of an old temple, faraway in space, but here and now to my present mind...

and now I am here, so very far from that land, and I am an echo of myself, years later: and I sit here in the great song of time, with a view of the sun going down, over the trees and the River Mole, and I write:

pink –
the great sea
of sunset:
worlds are born,
the moon, stars

and the moon is here again, radiant hallucination, in the transience of things, and yet it binds my worlds together and spans all the years with a bridge of light that glows in this autumn sky, linking the moments:

'the Interpretation
of Dreams' –
temples of light
a mountain peak
moons

and I can hear the music of Bach, its architecture and levels
and its structures of being: it is the

rapture of being alive, in holy dream, the music a sacred
continuum coursing through the millennia like energy: I hear
arias of tears and sorrow, arias of joy and the sublime, I think
of all those I have lost, and the worlds to which I have
belonged, and the old temples that rise in the moonlight, or
starlight, the earth blue in solar distances, and space with
those endless waves of light:

late evening – the moon:
after
the Mass in B minor
star after star
after star

and there in that land faraway, it was a world of light arranged
as flowers, and in that world I felt the presence of holy stones,
set down in a temple garden of combed sand or gravel, and I
have seen the silent ghosts of Nagasaki, how they once begged
for water, this their dying wish remembered in a fountain of
peace, and I've been to the Grand Shrine of Ise with its curving
wood more beautiful than any wood I have ever seen, and the
holy island of Miyajima, its orange gateway rising from the sea
like a sign, a land of volcano and pagoda and flowers of fire, a
land of spirits, lanterns and meditations – there amidst the
blue glass of skyscrapers, pink electric cities, plastic displays of
meals, beautiful ancient dances and the journey into the
masks of that old and sacred Noh Drama, the noise of
pachinko parlours and baseball grounds and Suzuki
motorcycles, a land of incense burning outside the Sensoji
Temple in Asakusa, where Kannon the goddess of mercy

resides, the old cone of Mt Fuji with those prints showing it in thirty-six views, that haiku dawn and tanka heart, the festival of O-Bon, when the glorious dead dance among us, the pink illuminations of the cherry petals that shine like glimpses or hints of eternity beyond, the temple bells of bronze that connect the worlds, the swords of steel and fire, those hostess bars, huge trees...

and I am sitting in my room now, and this is where I write my dreams, my memories, in a ceremony of light and shadow: and in this room, there is an arched white painted alcove, rounded over, an alcove of the floating world, with a haiku by Basho – impress of a stone at a temple in Japan – the Chinese characters flowing down the waxed paper like things alive: and there is a calendar showing scenes from old Kyoto, a temple with autumn crimson leaves upon the trees: and there is a print by Hiroshige, a picture of a snowy landscape, in blue and white, with a bent old man struggling over the bow of a bridge, over the river: and mountains: this is my perspective on the world: I am ready for the rest of my life: I go into the beautiful...

landscape
of the moon:
wild geese haunt
my grey dreams
with wings

this is where I am, this is where I am, my mind full, like a moon, shining, shining with memory, the sky of memory that is dreaming still, dreaming now in pink, or petals, of a landscape of dark temple wood, moonlight...

FINDING THE WORDS
by Kenneth Clelland

I am at a loss for words, as I watch the behaviour of the human race and being a member of it, makes it worse. I find myself being ashamed to be a human. The poem I wrote a couple of years ago, under my Hugh Timothy name entitled, *'Lest We Remember,'* pops back into mind, and I repeat it now, but purely as a starting point.

And still they die across the years
but worse by far we let them
as life by life is thrown away
then try not to forget them?

We feed the years of battlefields
with idealistic youth
who rallied to defend a cause
they're taught is total truth.
We may remember those who die
across each generation
rewarding each heroic act
with zealous veneration.

But dare we look with honesty
upon the reason why
we thought the cause could vindicate
the millions sent to die.
If one man dies through cruel mistake
we're strong in condemnation

but thoughts of millions lie beyond
attempts at contemplation

Can any cause the victor gains
bring justice for the sad remains?

I cast my imagining mind back and become one who is lying in the trenches. Another human being is running towards me. He is perfectly placed in my gunsight and my finger is tentative on the trigger of the gun braced tight against my shoulder. I have to decide whether I want to kill another human being. To snatch away his life. Can I justify taking the life of a fellow human? Is the fact that he has become maddened by war and if I don't kill him, he will kill me, a true justification? Have I the right to value my life over his. It isn't a matter of whether war can be justified because when it comes down to it, it is the man with his finger on the trigger, who has to make that decision. It is probably because we find this concept so troubling that we have switched ourselves to methods of remote war. When you press the triggers that shoot missiles, you don't have to look into the eyes of those whose lives you are about to take away.

I was adopted, but my natural father was a Canadian career airman flying with Bomber Command. He didn't have to look into the eyes of those that he dropped bombs on. Although, in those days, individually flown fighter planes that tried to stop you and you used your guns to defend yourself from them, brought a certain intimacy.

In my youth, at my school, you had a choice between joining the scouts or the cadet corps and at the age of 14 I learnt how to use the Lee-Enfield 303, a Sten gun and a Bren gun.

Militarily, it was a time of change, as such old weaponry was being replaced by modern semiautomatic rifles and we were taught the ins and outs of using those. Though still children, we were being instilled with the romance of being a soldier and we knew if we worked hard and took our army exams, Cert A part 1 and part 2, we could avoid the first year of square bashing on National Service.

It was the time of rise of the IRA, and it was known that they were attacking soft military targets to get hold of arms and ammunition and some of the boys in the cadet corps were guarding the school at night carrying guns from the school armoury, Lee-Enfield 303 rifles, actually ex WW1, loaded with live ammunition. And because the romance of the military had been fed to us, we all wanted to be one of them, defending our school. I missed National Service by a year.

My godson was an MA (medical assistant) in the army and was part of the forces fighting in the early days of the war in Afghanistan. He was first on the scene after a friendly fire attack by the Americans on a British Army unit. The sight he saw was to change him for the rest of his life. He described to me how he saw a British soldier with his chest blown off and yet his heart still visibly beating and knowing that there was nothing he could do about it and also knowing that this horror was inflicted by allies. He was physically shaking as he told me the story.

My own son loved the excitement of the outdoor life that the forces offered, and joined the Marines, but after initial training, he made the decision to take the option to leave. His commanding officer came down to see us, and to ask us if we could persuade him to stay on. He said that all the men liked him and he was an instinctive leader, which was just what they needed in a potential officer. We said we wouldn't interfere. It was his life, and therefore it had to be his decision. On one occasion, he said that it was being trained to be an instinctive killer that made him uncomfortable.

He worked in civilian life for a few years before making the decision to return to the Navy to be trained to become a senior MA. These have a higher level of qualification than army MA's as many smaller naval vessels do not have a doctor on board, the MA is probably the only person between you and God, if you become seriously ill. The senior MA can carry out minor surgery. He rose as high as his qualifications would let him. Later on, the Navy paid for him, to go to university to get a degree in environmental health. One day when a neighbour of his two doors down suffered a serious heart attack, my son was first on the scene and it was his work that saved the man's life. When for a while, he joined the ambulance service, his colleagues recognised his high level of qualification and frequently turned to him for advice. Here were positives that came out of working for the armed services.

Recently, the military has helped with various tasks over the pandemic. Another positive. But all focused on constructive behaviour rather than destructive. It strikes me that you have to be a fairly ruthless personality, if you are going to succeed in the army or the police. So, it is not surprising that elements within both are capable of creating less than desirable events.

It is probably, with the most honourable of intentions, that people go into the career they choose, perhaps, the military, the police, banking, government and politics, but they become embedded in an established and deep-set indoctrinated environment with which they either comply or have to change careers. Straightjacketed like that makes changing the world unlikely.

Humanity's biggest enemy is itself and therein lies the essence of its extinction. The dinosaurs lasted millions of years before their extinction. I doubt that the human race will survive a fraction of that time. The pandemic has shone a bright light on many of the exceptional people who could change our world. But it has also shone an equally bright light on the darker side of humanity who lack the wit to embrace what is good. The potential for the human race to blossom and shine exists, as does the potential for it to destroy itself. Sadly, the lunatic is incapable of seeing his own insanity.

It is a mad, mad, mad world now.

At 79, I think it is highly unlikely that I shall live long enough to see which path humanity takes, for I seriously believe that now is the moment that humankind has to get off the fence and commit humans to kindness, compassion, understanding and empathy with their world.

So, my message to my fellow humans is 'Good luck to you all. It's up to you now. I'll be off soon.'

DOMESTIC BLISS
by Peter Cates

I sit in peaceful reverie, in pipe and slippers mode.
Idly through the window, I note that it has snowed.
My gaze returns to fire's lure, smug with its buttery glow.
In the kitchen is my love: preparing our Christmas fare.
Her face is pink and glistens, her eyes have a glassy stare.
There is a rising clatter, as she ministers to her task.
"Do you need a hand?" Innocently, I ask.
From within the culinary din, comes a piper's dying skirl.
"What's that my dear?" .... Oh!
"And f*ck you, as well!"

THE BACON SANDWICH
by Peter Cates

Taste buds swell with lascivious delight
In anticipation, of that first bite.
But as my eager teeth sink in
And Piggy's fat anoints my chin,
I see him take his last muddy wallow
and remorse forbids me his flesh to swallow,
But then I reason he'd have died, in vain.
So, conscience eased I start to chew again.
Soon I masticate for all I'm worth.
Thinking, 'my, there's no better taste on earth.'
Then reflectively, as I the last morsel chew,
Give thanks, I'm not a Muslim or a Jew.

LIGHTLY DUSTED
by Corky Gormly

Hello. My name is Clarice. Yes really. No, I've never met another one in real life either. My father's grandmother was called that, and I got named after her. You can call me Rissy, everyone else does. You have to develop a sense of humour early on, with a name like mine. Clarice Caine. Now there's not a lot of people know that. He's said he never said that, but we all think he did. Michael Caine. A bit like the line in Casablanca. We all think it's 'play it again Sam'. We're wrong. It was just 'play it, Sam'. But, coming back to my namesake, I just wish I had Michael Caine's eyelashes. Gorgeous. Have a look, next time you see him in some of his early films.

Anyway, we were round at Tamara's, me and Mandy, sitting around her kitchen table. You should see her kitchen – stunning. I first met Tamara at the local pub, we all used to go there for years, from when we were about 17. That was where I met everyone round here. It was great – everyone talked to everyone else – a proper pub. It didn't matter if you were a biscuit salesman, tractor driver, actor or cancer research professor, young or old, we all got along.

There was one man who used to go in there a lot – George. Worked up in London in advertising, a creative. I saw a black and white photo of him once, when he was a lot younger – a proper portrait photo. He looked like Marlon Brando. George is a truly wonderful man. Kind, generous and so funny. If George was in the pub, we always had a better time. He had these stories he used to tell, and it didn't matter how many times you'd already heard them, you wanted him to tell them again, because of the expressions in his face, the different accents and voices, and of course, the story itself. Honestly, you'd be crying with laughter. We'd all stand around him and he'd be off, putting on a performance, enjoying every moment, laughing himself, and ordering bottles of champagne for people. He has a very mellifluous voice, deep and resonant. He's from the East End originally, a proper character. My favourite is his 'baked bean' story. No, it's not about farting, if that's what you're thinking. You'd never guess in a million years, and to be honest, I could tell you it, but you need George to tell you really. It's true, that line, isn't it? 'It's the way they tell 'em'. And besides, it's his story, not mine.

But I digress. Not that there's anything wrong with that. I like to think it's a sign of an intelligent mind – a brain with so many connections and neural pathways that you can't help going off at a tangent, making new links all the time. They said for years that our brain cells die off at a very rapid rate as we get older, but I have some comforting news. A neuroscientist called John Morrison has debunked that myth. They only die if you have something wrong – not if you're healthy.

But I'm doing it again, digressing. Let me tell you a bit more about us. We're in our 50's now, most of us. Some haven't quite reached that milestone yet. Tamara, the one with the stunning kitchen, is married to Nick. I can't remember how they met. She's short, even shorter than me, and I'm only 5'2". I think she's only 4'11". Anyway, her husband Nick is tall, Australian. He might have been in the navy at some point – I'm sure I've seen him somewhere in a photo in a white uniform, tanned and blond and gorgeous. He wasn't super rich when they met, I don't think (I'm not totally sure about that), but he is now. They moved to Monte Carlo, so I don't see them anymore. He does something in corporate law. They still have their house in Surrey, somewhere near Eric Clapton, I think. That's where we were at the time, in their house in Surrey. None of their children were at home any more. "Empty Nesters' as they say. Tamara didn't need to work, not for money that is. But she did a lot of volunteering, she's a kind person.

We were talking about affairs, and drinking wine. Wondering if our husbands had had affairs, and how we would know. Don't include me in this by the way, I'm not married. I don't know why. But I've had plenty of experience of unfaithful boyfriends. To me it's not worth it, not worth the hurt and the angst, I'm a loyal person. It's funny, isn't it? How you can be loyal to your normal friends easily, but not necessarily to your main 'loved one'. I often think we're seeking that same unconditional and selfless love from our partners, that we had from our parents. Assuming we had loving parents that is. I did. That gives you a strong foundation for life. That's what I believe.

But back to the story. Tamara was telling us about something that happened at work. She can't help but make you laugh. She has that sort of inner energy and zest for life that makes her eyes twinkle and she also has a humorous mouth – if you understand what I mean by that? It makes you want to smile expectantly, even before she's even said anything. We were wondering what signs you should look out for if your husband is having an affair. Taking a greater interest in their appearance, never letting their mobile out of their sight, working unusually long hours, things like that. Cutting short conversations. Answering 'oh, wrong number' when asked who was calling. Being a bit grumpy and short-tempered. Saying 'no, nothing's wrong', that sort of thing. She was saying she wouldn't ever really know if Nick was having an affair, because he's always away on business trips, and works incredibly long hours. Not that it's only men who have affairs, of course.

We were saying – wouldn't it be great if you could be a fly on the wall? I've always thought that. Haven't you? I suppose that was the concept for Big Brother, but the trouble is, once people know they're being watched they put on a performance, and don't act naturally.

It was something that Nick said later when he arrived home and we all had dinner, that gave me the idea. Nick was talking about one of their corporate parties they'd had recently, to celebrate their 40th year of business. They'd pulled out all the stops, hired a fabulous venue in London and organised some 'living statues' (practically nude, not like the ones you see in Victorian clothes in Covent Garden). Tamara didn't go. She hates those sorts of work events. They decorated a grand staircase, and it was easy to assume they were real statues, and not even look at them properly, until one moved a tiny bit, or their eyes flickered. I wish I'd been there, to see them for myself. They must all have had beautiful bodies I expect. Muscular, or toned. Or both. Young, and not a bit saggy and wrinkly around the edges, like most of us get as we get older. All sleek lines and magnificence.

Tamara started prancing about, pretending to be the statue 'The Thinker'. We were all laughing. I said to Nick – wow – I'd love to have seen those – what colour were they? Nick said they were silver, not heavily coated, but 'lightly dusted'.

I couldn't stop thinking about the living statues when I got home. I couldn't quite imagine what they looked like. I rang Mandy the next day. I haven't even told you about Mandy yet. Have I? She was a fashion buyer for Harrods. Now she does a bit of wholesale and showroom stuff. Not full-time. She's the one – she'd look right as a living statue. She's obsessed with physical fitness and diet. Not in a boring way. Just in a very healthy way. Legs to die for, seriously. Amazonian physique, sleek, smooth, strong, barely an ounce of fat. Just recently separated from her husband, I think that the main reason was they didn't have much to say to each other really. He was more interested in the children than in her, which is nice in one way, but not exactly right for a good relationship between them. I asked Mandy if she remembered the living statues conversation. I said I was going to investigate it a bit more, it had captured my imagination.

Later on that week we met up again, the 'girls', me Mandy, Tamara, Joyce, Debbie and Celestine. Yes, she's French, and I'm sure her name means 'heavenly'. She is divinely beautiful, put it that way, and she still has her French accent, even though she's lived here for years. She's been having some serious health issues; she had thought she'd got over breast cancer, but now they'd found it had come back. They were hopeful they could get on top of it again, but it was a very nasty surprise for her. Her husband died in a motor bike accident years ago, it was all very sad. Tragic. No children. We try to meet with her once a week to cheer her up, and show her some support, particularly at the moment. She always tries to be positive, and we all love her company. She has a great sense of fun – I think that has got her though all her bad times. She's a writer – she writes a lot of copy, and PR stuff.

Joyce is from Nigeria originally. That's another thing – she's the oldest of our group, but her skin just doesn't look old! Not at all. Black, with bronze highlights – almost like polished wood. She's in pharmaceuticals, helping develop vaccines. Yes, very topical I know.

She has the best laugh, booming and rich. She's very joyful and tactile, always cuddling you and kissing you. She's happily married, with three grown-up children now. Then there's the lovely Debbie – she's from Essex. Salt of the earth. Close family. Lovely husband, gorgeous children – she goes running with her daughter Beth – they look like two friends, rather than mother and daughter. She works supporting her husband with his business as a builder. And yes it's true – builders always seem to have fabulous homes.

So that's our little group. I haven't told you what I do have I? I work in an art gallery. So much variety, very interesting. You can make anything interesting – did you know that? Trust me, it's true. Actually, I never trust anyone who says 'trust me', do you? Anyway, we were in the pub and chatting with Tamara about Nick. She was saying she thinks he is definitely having an affair, and how she didn't know what to do next. Hiring a private detective was mentioned, but none of us knew any, or what they would cost.

And that's when I hit on my big idea.

Nick's chairman was going to host a 60th birthday party in London for all the people at the firm. Spouses could go, but Tamara had never enjoyed going to those kinds of things. The theme was going to be 'jungle' because his chairman is a very keen environmentalist. A bit like Sir Christopher Ondaatje. I love that. I wish more seriously influential or rich people became environmentalists, because if we don't have a healthy planet to live on, what have we got? That's how I see it. Because of the success of the 'living statues' at the previous event, Sir Christopher was planning on having them again, but this time, they would be jungle animals.

Without thinking, I said – why can't we be the fly on the wall as the living statues? We can spy on Nick, and he won't know it's us!

There was a pause, and a 'yeah right' type of reaction. And the conversation might have moved on, and we could have immediately forgotten all about it, except that Celestine said how much she would love to do something so completely different, which would take her out of herself, and focus on something other than her health and her work.

So that was it - we decided we would do it - for Celestine, for Tamara, and for us all!

Then we started to go 'hang on, wait a minute' as we began to think of all the practical things, like how do you stand still for so long, not laugh, and who paints your body; what with, and who makes the costumes?

"I have an idea", said Celestine. "Why don't we enroll on a yoga class that focuses a lot on meditation, and stillness? We could learn a lot there. And I'm sure we could find an artist who would paint our bodies, and develop some costumes for us!"

That sounded good, a great start.

"I wonder if it tickles?" said Debbie. "… when you're being painted, I mean. It might feel rather nice. And if you were being a jungle animal, you wouldn't feel embarrassed, because you'd be so disguised, no-one except us would know who we were!"

"I have to be a monkey" said Tamara, skipping sideways with her arms hanging down low, then rubbing her (rather rounded) tummy, making oooh ooh ooooh noises.

"Mandy could be a totem pole!" Joyce said. Mandy liked that idea.

"She's got that statuesque shape already!" Joyce continued. "I think I'd like to be a panther – I can slink and slide along, all glossy and beautiful!"

"What will you be Rissy?" asked Celestine. I think you could maybe be a koala bear – you have the right shape!"

To be fair, I'm quite a cuddly shape – I liked the idea of a koala.

"And you, Celestine? What about you?" I asked.

"Mmm, I'm really not sure. I think it would be great fun to be painted in tiger stripes – what do you think?"

We all agreed that was a great idea. That only left Debbie. We all looked at her expectantly.
"I have to be a lion. We must have a king of the jungle, and I love the idea of wearing a huge mane! Roooooaaarrrrrrr!" So, it was decided.

Except there was a bit of a snag. Surely, said Debbie, Nick's firm would hire the same troupe of living statues that had already been a great success? Well, apparently not. One of the statues had been rather indiscreet and unprofessional with one of the employees, so they were officially 'off the list'!

"I can say to Nick", said Tamara, "that I've come across this new troupe, and that they come highly recommended by Celestine, who has been doing their PR and knows all about them! And the party isn't for another 6 months, so we will have plenty of time to do what we need to do. I am sure I could persuade him to hire us. Celestine added that she would write some imaginary PR for us, say that she is now their agent!"

We paused for a moment, to let the whole idea sink in. Was it just a silly idea which, in the cold, sober light of day, would seem ridiculous and unachievable?

But the next day, Celestine had already found a yoga teacher who would come to Debbie's house twice a week, and help us stretch and relax, reduce our anxieties, become able to be more still, to focus and concentrate.

It was a very bonding session for us all. Calming, and time out to be ourselves, to still our racing thoughts. We looked forward to our sessions, and individually we each felt we were benefiting in different ways. Not least, strengthening our friendships as well as our bodies, and having a shared goal. It was fun.

Through my connections at the art gallery where I worked, I found a body paint artist and we met up and discussed our plans. Clearly, we'd need a mixture of costume and body paint. We told him what we wanted to be, and he said to leave it to him. Later, he did a run through and asked who'd like to volunteer, so we could see the result for ourselves? It had to be Mandy, as the totem pole.

By the time he had finished, she looked like a true work of art. Beautiful. The artist had chosen Australian aboriginal designs and colours. Together they decided she should wear knickers for modesty, which he painted over into his design, and to leave her top half naked. But the artwork didn't make her look naked at all – the shapes of her body were incorporated into the designs and became part of a whole.

We were silent in our admiration.

If Tamara also wore a wig, I am convinced that no-one would know it was her, even if they knew her really well.

I remembered how once I'd gone to a fancy dress party up in London when I was about 19. I didn't have any money for a costume, so I raided our bathroom (I think I must have just watched an old Boris Karloff Mummy movie at the time) for old bandages, got my mother to wrap me up tightly in them, with loads of safety pins, and got a lift to the party. What I hadn't realised was when I bent my elbows and knees, that yawning gaps would appear. What a disaster! I had something on my head and my hair was covered too. So, I was devastated when Bob from college said – 'Hi Rissy' as I arrived. Pausing with disbelief I asked how had he known it was me?

"The shape, I recognised the shape!" laughed Bob.

It was a word of warning to us all, we needed to make sure we were properly disguised!

… to be continued.

EVENING
by Diana Barclay

Shadows from the moonlight reflect upon our sphere,
And facets of bright diamonds in radiance appear,
We gaze toward our heaven and wonder fills our eyes,
Caught blindly for a moment in the splendour of the skies.

Deepest blue of softened velvet caresses every form,
To ease the pain of saddened hearts and comfort those who mourn.
Night perfume of soft aroma clings gently to the air,
While flickering rays of moonlight play amidst our hair.

Prisoners of the night-time, we cannot move or stray,
We stand transfixed in wonder to meet the coming day.

BABY... SOPHY
by Diana Barclay

She is my smile this baby cared by me,
Arousing passions never known before,
Eyes meet and quiet thought is understood,
I softly hum a lullaby to the child I adore.

So perfectly attired in every way,
Warm to the touch of love's embrace,
Relaxed and trusting in my helpless arms,
Complimented tiny form adorned in purest lace.

Her face is etched within my happy mind,
She is fast growing as swift days peel by,
I guide with all the love that I can build,
To meet her smile is more than words can say.

CHILDHOOD MEMORIES
by Diana Barclay

Remember my love, do you remember my sweetheart child?
How we played within our little room roughly styled.
We believed we were princesses dressed in netted silken gowns.
Our short cut hair was flowing gold to reach the lavish ground.
Splendid carriages gilt edged were drawn by healthy glowing
steeds,
Lithe bodies white with silver sheen, laced with diamond leads.
Our sweets became a banquet, a glass of orange became wine,
We were partnered by two princes, to reel with gracious line,
Floating, whirling, swirling round as feathers in the air,
The others at the party ball could only stand and stare,
Enchanted by our beauty, our soft rose pink attire,
Magnetic charm of innocence in them we warmed a fire.

Do you remember now my love, can you recall my sweetheart
child?
Games we thought reality, in our small room roughly styled.

PLASTIC, PAPER, TREE
by Sally-Claire Fadelle

Discarded mask lays on my lawn,
not mine.
Blown in from where?
Flirting with a crisp bag
old, tattered,
origin unknown.
They dance together a while.
In overgrown grass.
Rustling, crunching,
as wind's breath whispers
nature's tune animates.
Graceful pirouettes
percussion plastic – two Coke bottles
roll in tune under the gate,
touching then parting
taking separate sides
of my orchestra pit garden.
Landfill philharmonic.
Bag for life hovers
puffed up, inflated.
Stretched plastic.
flits from side to side
slowing
floating down
bounces
leaves.
Mulched remains.
Paper version of itself

A mourning dance.
Crow would stay with crow.

Plastic party moves on.
Under the hedge
Coke bottles roll
disappear.
Mask and crisp bag take flight,
with bag for life.
A few more rains
our paper friend,
will leave without trace,
or track
instead to return,
to the earth.
Curious Dorito bag drifts by,
Pauses.
Our paper mushy lays limp.
Gently!
Plop!
Recycling seemed kindest.
Deserving to be reborn
a notebook perhaps
like this one
but would rather be a tree.

GILDING THE LILY
by Justine John

PROLOGUE

She stood solemnly at the graveside. A single tear ran down her cheek. A man and a woman stood either side of her, and a younger man opposite. They all looked down at the expensive coffin being lowered in to their family plot. A few other mourners were scattered around; they formed a small, sad crowd, as the priest said the familiar burial prayer. But she barely heard the words as the coffin settled with an audible thump.

"... commit her body to the earth, for we are dust and unto dust we shall return..."

She looked around her. It was a warm, bright day in September, but there was an unusual wind – a hurricane was forecast. There were many head-stones here, and a few statues. Of angels mainly. Different colours but somehow the same hue. A few trees lined the perimeter fence, some bare, some evergreen. Beyond them the city buzzed – it went on with its day and didn't notice anyone missing.

The woman next to her was wearing a hat that didn't suit her. It kept catching the breeze and the woman's gloved hand caught it each time. It was annoying. She should have pinned it or something. She shivered as a gust blew by them and then smiled inwardly. How was it she came to be here? How was it that it all went so well? Was it her own cleverness, or was it luck?

"...the Lord lift up his countenance upon her and give her peace. We ask this through Christ our Lord. Amen."

"Amen", she joined in.

Amen indeed, she thought to herself. The relief was immense. The day after it happened, it flooded through her. How was it she had become capable of such a thing? And now, it was a huge secret.   But she had always been good at keeping secrets. It was over now. She could get on with her life.

"The Lord be with you."

"And with your spirit." everyone replied together.

Another gust.   She felt it curl around her stockings.   The woman next to her snatched at her hat.

"God of the living and the dead, accept our prayers for those who have died in Christ."

She wiped away the tear. The young man opposite caught her eye and sympathetically smiled. She smiled back in a way that said 'yes, I'm ok, thanks.'

And she was ok.

"Let us pray."

They bowed their heads, some held hands and some sniffed as they all solemnly recited the Lord's Prayer.

Her mouth moved as she mumbled the words but her thoughts were still elsewhere.

It was thrilling what had happened. And justifiable. She wondered if she could do it again. But the need would never arise, of course. She now understood how others could do it. This criminal act. How other people could get away with it. If she could do it, anyone could. How many people could be getting away with it right now? Thousands, millions? Was the city beleaguered with people crawling around getting away with their sins?

"Gracious Lord, forgive the sins of those who have died in Christ."

It was easier than she thought. That's what surprised her the most. It was just a matter of thinking it through carefully. Planning well. Did this make her a bad person? She was still the same inside. She was still capable of love, big love, and still wanted to be loved in return. Isn't that what life is all about – what everyone wants? And she felt more… worthy… or worldly, perhaps that was a more appropriate word. She felt more 'something' anyway, and that could only be a good thing. To feel more. To be more understanding of other people, and why they do things. Yes, she was still a good person – in fact a better person. It's not as if she didn't know the difference between right and wrong. What she did was wrong, but also right. She had righted the wrong. It felt good.

"Kindle in our hearts a longing for heaven."

There was a sudden movement from the woman next to her as her hat actually blew off. The woman made a quiet apology as she ran gracefully to the point where it had landed. The wind allowed it to stay there, and she picked it up, before returning to her place in time for the next Amen.

"Amen".

"Lord, have mercy."
Would anyone else forgive her if they found out? Or just God?

She looked for the words in her booklet and joined in again: "...raise us from the death of sin unto the life of righteousness..."

Righteousness? What is righteousness, really? A state of mind? A quality? A knowledge that one is morally correct? What she'd done was morally correct, even though it could be termed bad. So, it was righteous. She stood a little straighter. A small movement. Yes, it was righteous. She was righteous.

"May the love of God and the peace of the Lord Jesus Christ console you and gently wipe every tear from your eyes. Amen."

"Amen" she repeated. Amen indeed.

THE 1%
by Andrew Jackson

My mother was murdered on the shores of the great lake, long ago. But at least she did not die alone.

Maybe our civilisation had grown too large, too complacent. There used to be billions of us, building upon each other in claustrophobic cities where you were forever touching at least one of your siblings, maybe a cousin or two, and the odd grandchild. We were a society of lovers, of risk takers. We never worried about whether we could support the children that flew from our loins in great sneezes. But we had hope in our offspring, a great drive to better ourselves. To reproduce, to grow our family, to be more than what we were.

It all changed one fateful morning.

We were used to the presence of the lifeform. It was a constant object in our lives, like the light that occasionally penetrated the cloudy film in the heavens. It moved amongst us, sometimes. It often sat with us, pensive by the lake. It seemed to call the rains, in the mornings, with a titanic cry from its mouth. Occasionally we would hear it, somewhere beyond our world. It would sing, and sometimes there would be other voices, speaking in its language. The voices sounded mechanical, hollow. They laughed a lot.

The creature often staggered in the evenings. It would open its mouth, and a gout of acidic liquid would plunge into the lake, sometimes to remain for days. The more daring of us chose to feast on these rare offerings. But I'd seen a dozen sisters die when the lake grew jealous and claimed the spatter for its own in a violent tsunami.

The day started out like any other. I was gathered around the serene waters of the lake with my family, and the commune at large. My sister had just given birth, and I was debating with my mother on what we should name them, when we heard the voices.

First, the familiar lifeform, shouting proudly. This was nothing new. It shouted at the robot voices, after all. But it was met by one of its kin, higher-pitched, and considerably louder. We noted this but thought little of it. I myself was heavily pregnant at this stage and had little time for lower life.
My daughters were born prematurely, forced out of me in fright, when the sky-door blasted open with a world-shaking crack. I was not the only one to experience this on judgement day.

The voice was deafening, the smaller of the two lifeforms towering over the lake shaking the familiar one by its appendage and roaring in its face. It appeared to recede for a moment as we looked on, as if it had given up, but quickly reappeared next to its compatriot, cradling a white object. The creatures looked vaguely similar, as if born from the same familial cluster.

Some of us were amused by the spectacle. My mother shuddered in silent laughter as the smaller life form thrust the object at the other and slammed the door behind it. Alone, the giant lifeform sighed, and rubbed an appendage over its face. It expelled gas in a great exhalation. Then it committed genocide.

My mother was amongst the first casualties as acid rain blasted in stinging white spurts from the maw of the great weapon our formerly benign companion turned on us. Those the acid touched did not scream. There was no time for that. The screams came from the survivors, who watched a family chain as long as the universe boil in their homes before their eyes.

The liquid coursed over and through me, a harsh bitter citrus that seemed to set my cell ablaze, seeping into my cytoplasm and blasting in white-hot waves against my membrane. But unlike my mother, I did not burst. The pain overrode my senses, and I mercifully missed the following assault.
I awoke to the sound of humming. A low, mournful dirge that suited the scene. The lifeform was sweeping the banks of the lake with a large porous block of something undulating and yellow, its lips moving as it scoured the traces of its war. Not that there was much left.

I prayed as it mopped, that it would sweep me up in its graveyard detail. Wring me out over the waters of the lake, now bubbling with a white hostility. Hopefully I wouldn't survive the journey down. I reached out for my mother, for my sisters, but I was alone on the rim, and fate was not done with me yet. The lifeform missed me.

For the first time in recorded history, the banks no longer sang with the voices of my people. Around me, spanning in twin curves to a sickening horizon was an expanse of sterile white. If I squinted my eyes, I thought I could see a speck on the far rim, another survivor, here with me at the apocalypse. But the tears made it hard to distinguish.

153

I reacted instinctively, as our kind have done for eons past. I tried to get pregnant. Reaching inside myself, caressing my wounded cell, encouraging it into its delicious division. Twin daughters would bring the smile that had faded with the loss of my last two, moments ago. But something was happening. Something brutal, something unholy. My body was refusing to obey me. The citrus poison inside me had sterilised me as it had our world. I wept as the lifeform whistled cheerfully to itself and walked away from its massacre.

Time passed. I am not sure how long. All I know was there was a lot of it. In my solitude, I turned away from the pain of my neutering and embraced study. I studied the giant creatures, their movements, their patterns of behaviour. Once I was rescued, I would need to show I had learned. That I knew how to strike back, avenge the countless victims lost to an act of high evil. I began to learn their language. It was stamped on their weapons. My eyes were weak by this point, from the tears shed for my race. Perhaps my voice was the last that could tell the tale, if there was anyone left to hear it. But all I could have said, in a tongue as alien as my solitude, was: Kills 99% of germs.

AFTER THE CLASS
by Margaret Graham

We'd done the stretching,
The breathing,
The relaxation.
We'd pictured colours – red to violet –
A spectrum, flowing through us.

We felt lazy now,
Ten of us,
Sitting on the flowered dining chairs,
In the lull before lunch.

The talk goes to and fro,
Across and around the circle.
Of parenthood
And the best age to have a baby.

"I was 28," says Gladys.
Rosemarie had two sets of twins
Before she was 30.
All have been married,
And Olive the newest widow.

Everyone has generations of offspring,
They visit Sundays, mostly.
Except for Olive.
It was just her and Stan.
Then just Olive.

"21's a nice age to have a baby," Olive says,
"That's how old I was."
We all agree. A nice age.
Olive smiles, another Mum among mothers –
Just for a week – but still a lifelong member.

A VISION – DREAMS & SHADOWS
by A A Marcoff

all the land – dream
all the waves of the sea – dream
all the world – dream
sutra after sutra – dream
a mantra – dream
all that I am – dream
all I ever will be – dream
butterflies – dream
the valley of bones – dream
a field of buttercups – dream
the wilderness – a dream
the tree of life – a dream
infinity – a dream
gulls – dreams & dreams
the song of a skylark – no more than a dream:
                    I think all dreams have wings:
& now here I stand
by the waters of this silence
at dawn – the tabernacle of all things wild –
                    becoming,
the shadow of a kingfisher
the shadow of time
the shadow of a dragonfly
the shadow of fire
shadow of butterflies
shadow of light

the shadow of stone
& the shadow of the mind
the shadow of a dream
the shadow of death
shadow of a shadow
the shadow of memory
& the shadow of a gull
the shadow of silence
shadow of the river
              slowly becoming itself
        as once it was
          in another life of dreams:
& as I sit in a field
              with the dandelions
turning slowly into time
I know I know I will never ever wake from this dream
& it is a dream set in stone
in the eternal dream of the sun
& its everlasting world
of shadows

CONVERSATION
by Judy Apps

We scour the bottom of the pan
For subjects mutual, topics of compatibility,
I ask what it is you do?
You talk and number tasks, accountabilities.
Yet there is skill and movement there
Which opens the door a chink; with hint
of your desires and loves, blows wider still
Until at length, perceiving where you stand,
The rock that bears your structure up,
Its sense and purpose in your world,
I look you in the eye, you mine.

Dissolving in those pools we join
And could have looked and joined before
Had I allowed myself to stand
In me upon this spot and let you in.
But welcome now. Connection's in the glance
Of an eye and spreads to gut and soul,
A deep spring overflowing touching both,
A look, a breath, and we as one.

WHEN THE GRAPE MEETS THE WEATHER
by Jill Benson

Presented myself for grape-picking (Pinot Noir) at the Manor. As soon as I got out of the car, was given the once-over by a large, black, bony-headed labradoodle, who rather thought he'd like to get in my car!

The work was okay, but a bit monotonous, and hurt my neck. Was covered in sticky, red grape goo early on. Excellent lunch, where last year's (the first) rose was plentiful, followed by home-made cake *et al.* (How will we pick grapes, if we are all pissed?!) Marianne and John, (delightful lord and lady of the manor), were excellent, and very hands-on, hosts. He is an ex-hedge fund manager, and was just off to Africa when we met. When I asked, casually, about the nature of his trip, he replied simply: "Development". I discovered later he is involved with building schools in Africa. They are a great couple, and take their part in the local community very seriously, which is why I wanted to support them.

Some of my co-workers were, (in their own words) 'ex-colonials', brought up in Kenya, with parents who were of the time depicted in the film, "White Mischief", which majored on coke-sniffing and the general decadence of certain members of the upper classes. The nice lady I met was rather sceptical about the veracity of the film. Interestingly, she was adamant about Lord Mountbatten's role as 'fixer' in the marriage of Queen Elizabeth and Prince Philip.

Some of the other ladies - self-styled *grande dames* of Surrey - talked about their grandsons' polo ponies quite a lot. Somebody else's grandsons talked of nothing but their exam results. Rather tedious.

However, during the course of the day, I learnt a few interesting facts about viniculture. Rod, the head gardener, told me that badgers adore grapes and, once they start taking the grapes, it's time to harvest! (And, the badgers wait until the time is right.) I asked him whether it might be possible to "turn" the badgers and get them working on our side. A bit of partnership working, perhaps?? He smiled politely, and continued picking, looking up at the rain clouds.

Prior to all this, in an effort to try and identify the grape 'thieves', Rod set up night cameras. He laughed as he described the size of the very large badger's bottom, as the animal squeezed through a very small hole in the vineyard fence. Foxes are also partial to grapes, I learnt.

Unfortunately, the vines are stricken by botrytis, so progress is terribly slow, as we had to winkle out the bad stuff, and then stamp on it to stop the virus leaching into the soil.

By the end of the day, my right wrist is stiff, and my hands are soaked in sweat and goo, and have turned green - the colour of the gloves. Reminds me a little of picking apples and pears in Upper Galilee in the 1970s. (Though it's an awful lot cooler.) But Marianne and John are a great deal more caring than my kibbutzniks were!

For some reason, I was assigned to vines all day which were far away from everyone else, which got a bit lonely and boring. But it was satisfying when, at last, I met my co-workers halfway along the vines, and we finished the line together.

And then it was all over, and the young gardeners, and John's sons, loaded the trays of grapes onto a small truck, to be taken immediately for pressing to another larger, local vineyard.

More marvellous cake and coffee was proffered, as we relaxed and chatted, glad to have got in the harvest before the rain - which was just starting. Looking out over the vineyard, Marianne pointed out young elms they have planted, now turning yellow. Because of the ravages of Dutch Elm disease, many of us would have had difficulty identifying these trees.

Well... as days go, it was certainly different, and I'm glad I gave it a go. After all, I heard on the grapevine, as it were (!), the other larger, local vineyard makes you PAY to pick grapes!!

SPRING IS A HARP
by Sally-Claire Fadelle

Through the veil a harp,
can you hear it?
distant shores,
sea lapping in time,
memories to be made waiting
for summers horizon.

A harp closer now,
its pulse echoes transition,
shifting slowly,
from Winter to Spring,
unfolding sweetest sound
intricate tunes dainty,
dance gently on my shoulder.

I shake off a layer,
old skin shedding,
a final pirouette of shivers
fall gracefully to my feet,
toes still enjoying warmth of wool.
sun peering tentatively,
through puffs of cloud,
delicate blue silk ripples,
clothes the sky,
in finest cloak sheer,
grass glitters at first dawn,
tiny droplets
winter's remaining dew,

twinkle like precious diamonds,
on velvet gown of green,
patchwork in recovery.
open windows,
invite Earth's breath in,
to play,
to share a land coming out of darkness,
feel it,
for Spring is close now,
ever so close.

harp picking notes,
floating ~ lingering,
they rise gently,
then fall ~ touching,
stroking the Earth with magic,
waking sleeping trees.
who lift bare branches,
yawning bulbs ~ buds,
stretch roots,
slowly pushing through softening soil ~ rich,
as colour revives.
dreams of long days,
returning friend,
a child to be fed ~ nurtured,
listening to a heartbeat,
growing stronger ~ louder,
steady rhythm.

my harp,
soul of a wizened sage ~ ageless,
beauty of a nymph ~ agile,
frolicking ~ prancing,

on winter's bed,
on hibernating creatures,
returning birds,
gathering them for the feast,
on the lush, living carpet,
of daisies, Buttercups,
bluebells, Forget-me-nots,
promises reverb,
soft notes ~ on wood ~ organic,
fragile Earth cleansed ~ rebirth,
inner strength ~ fortitude,
nourishing,
vibrations of hope,
happiness,
lightness,
ring together
through tender strings ~ inspiring,
for Spring is close now,
ever so close.

birdsong dovetails,
white plays outside my curtained windows,
flickering through voiles,
teasing me out of sleep earlier
and earlier, my waking hour,
days pass,
my harp fades ~ yielding
to fresh sounds coming alive ~ purest acoustics,
fingers hover,
barely touching strings,
first time lover,
feeling their way ~ unsure,
weaving tenderly,

endless tapestry of love,
colours melding ~ moist,
softest down.

hurrying by ~ a butterfly,
heart shaped wings ~ whisper,
I love you,
a faint harp plays ~ in duple,
timeless pavane,
retiring wind ~ leaves flutter,
petals sway,
embraces ~ in gossamer breeze,
beaming sunshine,
to a new-born season,
a kiss brushes my cheek ~ speaks,
Spring is close now,
ever so close.

LAST NOTES
by Pauline Watson

Melancholy, notes are lost
sad, lonely, past times
memories, notes spiraling
out of control, dark times
bleak sounds
lost in the blues.

Notes flickering, lingering
held by ivory keys
drums skittering
metal brushes on skin
filter of sounds
floating.

Syncopation pounding
twisting sounds
metre, theatre, clash
of notes. Saxophone
sweet as sugar
that's jazz.

BIOGRAPHIES

Alison Allen

After leaving teaching in 2016, Alison Allen did an MA in Creative Writing and is now enjoying the chance to write full time. She has had stories and poetry published in various magazines and online sites and her current work-in-progress, a YA novel, was longlisted in this year's Mslexia novel competition. Exploring the countryside and investigating the past form the inspiration for much of her work.

Peter Cates

As a lover of the English language, I originally joined Phoenix writers in the hope of expanding and diversifying the type of poetry, that I usually wrote. This being the emotive 'woe is me' type. I don't feel I have fully achieved my objective. Yet! But my enjoyment of the monthly Phoenix meetings, has certainly encouraged me to carry on trying.

Corky Gormly

Corky Gormly is a fledgling writer, and self-employed ex-advertising agency qualitative researcher. She lives quietly in the Surrey countryside enjoying all the beautiful Surrey Hills scenery and wildlife. Her hobbies are walking, playing with her dog and socialising.

Richard Howard

Short stories have always been my preferred form. Many have been inspired by my interest in, and experience of, ghosts and uncanny experiences. I've self-published two books and am currently collaborating on a screenplay of my story, 'Flora's Return', which is my sequel to Henry James' novella The Turn of the Screw. www.richard-howard.com

A A Marcoff

A A Marcoff is an Anglo-Russian poet who has lived in Africa, Iran, France and Japan. He has worked as a university librarian, a teacher, and an OT Helper in a large psychiatric hospital, where he was in charge of poetry and creative writing. A long-standing member of the international haiku and tanka community, he has had longer poetry published in many journals, including Poetry Review, Ambit, Agenda and Fire. He lives near the beautiful River Mole.

Jill Benson

Jill is a published poet, short story writer, diarist and radio reviewer. As a secretary on The Times, she was fired with an ambition to write and, subsequently, became a sub-editor for IPC Magazines. She has had a variety of jobs, from chainsaw assistant to working in a public library. Recent work includes features and reviews for e-paper, Guildford Dragon, Age UK magazine and South East Rambler. She is a skilled interviewer, and also enjoys contributing to R4 programmes.

Tim Jenkins

Timothy Jenkins has been a member of Phoenix Writers' for nearly 24 years and ran the group as Chairman for 18. He writes Poetry as Hugh Timothy and prose and plays as Kenneth Clelland. Some of his poems have won prizes in international competitions and his plays have been performed and scripts filmed. He ran a fringe theatre company in London in the late 90s.

John Lemon

After reading Law at Oxford, John did a ten-year stint in the Home Office before going back to university to read English. After that he worked in education, including teaching English and Creative Writing at Surrey University. In his spare time, he edited the poetry magazines Retort and was artistic director of the High Street Theatre Company. He is now retired, insofar as anyone with a daughter and three small grandchildren can ever really be retired.

Justine John

Justine is Chairman of the Phoenix Writers' Circle. In 2016, after thirty years in corporate life in London, Justine John decided to take a chance to write the novel that was 'in her' since she was a child. Gilding the Lily is the result of this and since then two more books are in the pipeline currently. She lives in the Surrey hills with three horses, two dogs, two donkeys and a husband! More info here: www.justinejohn.co.uk.

Wendy Freeman

I am a founder member of two writers' clubs, and joined Phoenix in 2015. I enjoy performance poetry. I write poetry and fiction for children and adults. I have had poems published in anthologies such as Montage and Montage 2.

Sally-Claire Fadelle

Sally-Claire is a writer and dreamer. She writes poetry, fiction and non-fiction. She has read her work regularly at events across the Southeast. She studied creative writing at the University of Chichester. Sally-Claire has been published in anthologies. Writing is her second love, her first being windmills. She has a poetry collection coming out and is working on a novel. She hopes to one day live in a windmill, eat cake, and write a lot.

Lena Walton

Lena Walton holds down two jobs yet still finds time somehow to write. Her first novel Jewish Days Arab Nights was self-published on Amazon in 2014. She is preparing the sequel Not Quite Gaza for publication this year. And her latest endeavour is a dark psychological thriller called The Dark Side of the Hill.

Andrew Jackson

Andrew Jackson writes primarily science fiction, thriller, and horror. Born and raised in Leatherhead, Surrey, he grew up on Star Trek, Alien, and videogames he was too young to play. His debut science fiction novel is in the works. His poetry has been published in Asylum, a magazine specialising in mental health awareness. Samples of his work can be viewed online at andrewsfiction.com.

Margaret Graham

Margaret Graham, previously best known for her writing on 'chair' yoga, (Keep Moving, Keep Young: Gentle Yoga Exercises for the Elderly) is now a successful playwright for amateur theatre. In 2014 and 2016 Ifield Barn Theatre's productions of her 1960's sell-out comedy/dramas - Miniskirts & Revelations; then sequel Flowery Shirts & Strange Relations - received NODA awards. Thought-provoking Benches followed in 2017 and farce Rita's Revenge in October 2019.

Judy Apps

Judy Apps is a TEDx Speaker (How Your Voice Touches Others – the true meaning of what you say – at TED.com), and author of five books on communication, including The Art of Communication (Capstone) and bestselling The Art of Conversation (Capstone). She is published in 11 different languages. She writes regular articles on everyday matters at judyapps.co.uk; loves family and friends, singing and countryside and is interested in the state of the world - as a late developer!

Diana Barclay

Diana grew up in London and has a daughter, Sophy. After writing poetry from aged eleven and turning down drama school to work with children, she settled in Reigate and trained in aromatherapy and reflexology. Her work includes illustrated poetry for children some of which has been exhibited in the Royal Academy of Fine Art.

Jess Newton

Jess fell into writing as a teenager, tempted by the dark world of fanfiction. She dabbles in science fiction, fantasy and romance, always with queer characters at the centre of the action. Her stories are the ones she wished she could have read as a teenager, when she often struggled to find characters, she could identify with. Her first book, Posterity, is due to be published by Gurt Dog Press in winter 2021.

Pauline Watson

Pauline Watson, now retired, concentrates on gardening and writing. Member of Mole Valley Poets, and Phoenix Writers. She has been successful in poetry competitions, and her work has been included in poetry anthologies. She plans to publish a book of her poems later this year.

Rosie Basten

Rosie is a poet and fictional prose writer. She has written since she was a child and has a deep love for metaphor and contrast, both of which often present themselves in her writings on nature, relationships and fantasy folklore.

Nicholas Mackey

Nicholas Mackey is a writer, photographer and traveller – on a perennial journey. As a writer, happy to work in fiction, non-fiction and poetry. As a photographer, in relentless pursuit of timeless imagery. Currently writing a travelogue on Northern Mesopotamia following a recent visit to Turkey. Former teacher, bus conductor, hop picker, film director, entrepreneur, aviation IT analyst and journalist. British/Irish nationality; married with two sons.

You can find more information about Phoenix from the website: www.phoenixwriterscircle.co.uk

L - #0185 - 150921 - C0 - 210/148/10 - PB - DID3160953